THE RIM-WORLD LEGACY

F. A. JAVOR

N·A·L **SiGNET** BOOKS

A SIGNET BOOK

Published by The New American Library

SIGNET TRADEMARK REG. U.S. PAT. OFF. AND FOREIGN COUNTRIES
REGISTERED TRADEMARK—MARCA REGISTRADA
HECHO EN CHICAGO, U.S.A.

SIGNET BOOKS are published by
The New American Library, Inc.,
1301 Avenue of the Americas, New York, New York 10019

PRINTED IN THE UNITED STATES OF AMERICA

THE
RIM-WORLD LEGACY

PROLOGUE

I'm six-feet-four, weigh two hundred pounds, and swim about as well as a porous rock. All the same, I pressed myself down into the black water the sparse weeds sprang from, listening.

Listening. Straining my ears in the heavy darkness until I thought the skin on the back of my neck would pop. Knowing that the rise and fall of the sounds those who were after me were making was not in their nearness or distance, but in me.

Warily, swearing inside at the way the strength in my hands was coming and going, I started working away at the base of a tall reed.

Bending it. Pulling it down to me slowly, slowly, all the time aware to the point of torture that in the night-vision glasses the men tracking me were sure to be wearing, a movement, unless it be heartbreakingly slow, would show as a sudden flaring of bright yellow against the dull red of the overall background stillness.

"Pike," someone shouted, his voice coming at a low point in my hearing, but I could make out my own name well enough.

"Pike. Come out. Give yourself up. Don't make us come in after you."

Give myself up. There were children's and women's voices mingled with those of the men after me, and the sound of them added that thin frosting of urgency to my predicament that had me fighting to hold at bay the unreasoning temptation to break and run. Break and run and evade my pursuers by sheer animal speed.

Sheer animal speed against the animal thing after me. The thing that brought its women and children with it to the hunt. The thing that by this act revealed itself to me to be no policeman's posse that might be content to capture and to hold me. The thing that cried out to me to give myself up to it.

The thing that was a howling mob.

Panic tried to force its treacherous way into the racing of my mind.

I fought to hold it in check and kept pulling the reed down slowly, fearful that it would slip from my weakening hands and the motion of its snapping erect betray my location as surely as if I'd sent up a flare.

Fighting, for the same reason, the urge to shake my head to ease the prickle of the old scar I could feel throbbing on the top of my balding head. The scar that was a souvenir of the Second Police Action. Thin, almost invisible, it seemed to have a sensor of its own that made it tingle when it thought I was about to head into something that, if I was lucky, I'd live to regret.

And now at last I had the reed flat in the water and hidden, close to my body.

I began twisting it. *Slowly, slowly, but hurry, before they can rig and bring up the heat detectors that will use the warmth of your own body as a beacon to home in on.*

Twisting the reed. Swearing silently at my hands and their unsure grip that was making of so simple a task so formidable a project. Fighting to keep my lungs from gasping their air and make tremble the high grasses around me. Make them tremble and the motion betray me to my pursuers.

I felt the reed weakening and now it was free in my grasp.

I strangled my gasp of relief and, forcing myself to wait until I felt my grip on it firming, I broke off the tip. Then, raising one end to my mouth, I blew into it.

I blew, feeling my cheeks puff out and straining until the pinpoints of light danced red and yellow in my eyeballs and the strength of my lungs ebbed away.

Nothing.

The reed was plugged. *Membranes crossing its diameter.*

Pressed down in the chill water but sweating, I groped in the darkness for another reed. Thin, but sturdy.

I found one, pulled it down and worked it free as carefully as I'd done the first one even though now I could hear, dimly, and more clearly, and dimly again as my hearing phased in and out, the unmistakable beat of approaching hover-craft.

Hover-craft, heat-detecting units jerry-rigged on long cables to hang below them and sweep close to the water in their search for the warmth of my body. My head, my face would be enough.

Hover-craft, more than one from the sound, and sooner than I'd expected. They must be units commandeered from the spaceport that was the chief reason for *Poldrogi's* existence. The planet's city police could not have been cleared to move outside their jurisdiction so quickly. The men in those hover-craft would be as free of official control as the mob on the ground.

Hurry now, hurry, but do not move with anything but agonizing slowness lest your motion flare brightly yellow in the night-vision glasses of your hunters.

Using the thinner reed as a reamer, I poked into the larger one, first from one end and then from the other.

Again I blew into it and this time my breath was unobstructed. The inner passage of the long reed was clear.

Carrying my newmade tube, and stopping only when the drag of the water threatened to wrench it from my fingers, I groped in the darkness for deeper water. Oddly enough, even though no one, not even the SpaceNav experts back in my service days, had been able to teach me to swim, I had no particular fear of deep water. And even if I had, the racket of hover-craft, now clear in the night behind me, would have given me reason enough to press on.

From the sound of things, it was plain to me that I'd just about had all the time I was going to get to find out how deep the semi-swamps that were the lakes of *Poldrogi* could become.

I found a clump of weeds that felt a little thicker than the rest and, blowing through my reed to clear it, put one end among them so that it might the better escape the notice of my pursuers.

The other end of my reed I put into my mouth and, pinching my nose between my fingers as best as their phasing strength would let me, I let myself settle down, the black water closing over my head, plugging my ears with its characteristic roar, until I sat on the silted and treacherous-feeling bottom.

They would not come after me, I hoped, once they'd lost me in their night-vision glasses, until there was daylight enough to see me by.

I was lucky, I suppose, that this was *Poldrogi* and not Linedo or Parsi or any one of the more fashionable tourist planets that made of their scenery a feature, flooding it with lights that came on automatically at the approach of a human.

But *Poldrogi* was, after all, only a transit world. A place to transship cargoes or wait out starship connections and aside from the anticrime lights in the spaceport city itself, its Council of Peers was not one of waste power on lighting up the countryside.

All I could do for now was wait, knowing that the hover-craft, their heat detectors dangling beneath them, were crisscrossing over my head. Wait in the pulsing water and hope that my breath, traveling the length of the reed I'd selected, would emerge in a wisp cool enough to escape discovery.

A search robot, I knew, would not be commandeered, like a hover-craft, and sent in after me. They were designed to keep the starships and their cargo holds clear of stowaways and other unwanted visitors and would not function in deep water. But someone might think to search over their bills of lading in the hope that there might be in one of the shipments an android hunter on its way to a sporting world. And I could not hide from myself the knowledge that if it were activated and sent to ferret me out, I would stand no chance against a thing that only *looked* like a man.

I pushed the unsettling thought out of my mind. To give it play now, when I was over my head in water, trying to ignore the unseen things that bumped and slithered against me in the blackness, could only build the panic that would destroy me.

No. For now the only thing to do is to wait. Wait and try to think of how you got into this predicament in the first place. Then, maybe you will be better able to figure out what to do when you get out and away from here. If you get out and away from here. If . . . .

Stop. Stop thinking along those lines. Think of the girl.

The girl. She had been by the open transhaus window when I stepped in through the corridor door.

CHAPTER ONE

POLDROGI.

I came awake to the sound of a pounding on the panel at the side of my head and the sight of a sterile blue-green surface so close to my face as to seem to be pressing down upon me.

Bunk. I'm in my bunk, but I feel heavy; planet heavy. The grav units ... something wrong with the ship's grav units. Trouble ... the pounding in my ear. ...

And then I knew where I was. I shook my head and blinked, trying to clear my sleep-clogged nose and throat of the acrid chemical bite of the disinfected wash of air.

There were no grav units for something to be wrong with. The pull on my body was a natural one. I was not in my old bunk aboard the SpyEye IV, but in a *Poldrogi* transhaus sleep cubicle, and the pounding was being done by someone in the corridor outside my coffinlike enclosure.

I slid back the thin plastic panel. "What?" I said. "What do you want? My time's not up." I fumbled in the wall pocket behind my head for my wrist-chrono. "I've got two ... maybe three hours. ..."

The fat man standing in the corridor showed me his handmade *Poldrogi* teeth. "Lady to see you," he said, giving the first word the local accent that made it sound like "lead-y."

"Upstairs. My office," he said full into my face.

Lord. Do they even make their transhaus managers eat those miserable disinfectants?

I stared at his fat face peering in at me. Who knew I was here? Who even knew I was alive? Lady, he'd called her, and I knew transit-world locals well enough to know that if that's what he called her, then that was what she was, and not some corridor-walker trying to drum up a little trade with an ex-SpaceNav serviceman.

And with starship passage rates being figured not by the person but by the pound, anyone with *his* heft couldn't be anything but a local. Space warp technique or no, it still took

11

power and money to move a weight from one place to another. It would take plenty of both to move him.

"A lady?" I said. "For me? Are you sure?"

"She ask for pho-tographer. You it."

Photographer. Then she'd asked for me, not by name, but by business. It could mean she had a job she wanted done and it could also mean that she wasn't too sure how simon-pure an assignment it was. A lady with a clean photo job in mind didn't go down into a spaceport transhaus to find someone to do it for her.

She wasn't too sure about it, and she was looking for a photographer who needed the money.

I was a photographer ... and I needed the money. Lord, did I need the money. I could at least listen to what she had to say.

I pushed the panel all the way back and slid out of my cubicle. "Thanks," I said to the fat manager. "Thank you for calling me."

He showed me his hand-carved teeth again. "No thanks. You only one here. I tell lady you come."

I watched him shuffle away from me. He was broad, but then the corridor wasn't any wider than it needed to be and he just about filled it with his beam. The scuffs, the crushed shorts, the T shirt he had on may have had some color to them once, but the constant washing, the sterilizing that transhaus regulations called for had long ago bleached it out until now they looked to have been dipped in drying and faded blood.

It was clean, all right. It was cheap. But it wasn't fancy.

I snaked my travel jumpsuit out of the mesh bag at the back of the cubicle, shook it to free it of the wrinkles it had picked up, stepped into it. The zipper was stiff, its tab skimpy, but I managed to work it closed and stood for a moment wondering if it would look better if I took my cameras with me or left them until I'd heard what the woman upstairs wanted of me.

I snorted. Why be cute and pretend that my tongue wasn't hanging out for the job? If she didn't think I'd be eager, she wouldn't have come to this place. I glanced down at my low, tropicweight boots. They were travel-scuffed, badly, but did it matter?

I pressed my thumb against the lockplate of the safebox at the foot of the bunk-shaped cubicle, waited for the "ding" that would show that the print had been recognized and, when it came, raised up the narrow lid and lifted out my cameras.

My record unit. Smaller than a deck of cards, it stored its images on a coil of split-8 metallic foil and could shoot them individually or in a continuous strip that could run for eleven minutes at one exposure every half-second.

For light, it had twin electronic flashtubes, one behind each of the tiny windows at its upper corners. These could be fired individually or together, or set to go off alternately when the camera was set for continuous operation.

Shockproof, watertight, I used it for the things I needed to keep a record of or didn't want the bother of copying. Client agreements, setups I might need to repeat, ship schedules. It went into the zippered pocket on the left sleeve of my jumpsuit.

And my pretty camera. Correspondent type, but larger than most carried, I'd had it specially fitted with a pic-hold finder that let me see what I'd caught before I permanized the matching hologram record.

It had cost me all of my severance pay and a little extra, but at the time I figured it was worth it. A man is no better than the tools of his trade, that sort of thinking. And I did have high hopes of opening up the star-worlds with it.

Only the star-worlds didn't much seem to care if a balding, ex-SpaceNav Photo Mate opened them up or not. Everything within reasonable reach of my camera had already been more than thoroughly opened up or was being eyed by a major network so that, in my hunt for something fresh enough to jolt someone into an acceptance, I found myself drifting more and more off the beaten spaceways that had followed the population flow in toward the center of the galaxy, and farther and farther out along the loose spiral of its arms to where its rim trailed off into the intergalactic void.

That I should be the only photographer loose in a transit world transhaus did not particularly surprise me. *Poldrogi's* topside hostels were not particularly overlarded with swank, but they did have infinitely more appeal for men with firm contracts and expense accounts. Or even with paying contracts alone.

Automatically, and from long habit, I checked the charge of my recording chamber and of the short-pulse, low-intensity laser speedlight and its synchronized reference-beam emitter that nestled close up under the flaring and filter-

13

shielded hologram aperture, before I slung my camera by its strap around my neck.

I gave my sleep cubicle a final check to make sure I hadn't forgotten anything, gave the scar on my head a thorough rubbing that I hoped would last it for a while, and walked to the end of the narrow corridor.

Walked past the other cubicle panels, open and shut. It was more like walking through a mausoleum than a hostelry for the living. Walked to the end of the corridor and started up the spiraling ramp that led to the surface level and the fat manager's office.

CHAPTER TWO

The manager had his door slid back against *Poldrogi's* airless heat and I saw her standing at the open window opposite before I rapped on the scrubbed-white jamb.

She turned at the sound, moving with a suppleness that made my eyes automatically flick to the dark arch of her left eyebrow in search of the telltale, faintly glowing, lilac "A" that the law made mandatory.

It wasn't there, of course. Androids, even female ones, were around, but they were as expensive to buy and maintain as a privately owned spaceyacht. And just as likely to be out and unattended on a transit world.

My eyes, like any photographer's, explored the bones of her wrist as she held out her small hand to me. Knowing from their structure, under the real-fur bangle, that her ankles in those pipestem boots the women were wearing this season would be well worth the looking at.

"Mi-ister Pike? Mister Eli Pike?"

She spoke hesitantly, the delicacy of her voice matching that of her bones. Her Intragalactic English had an accent I couldn't quite place, yet somehow I seemed to sense in it an echo of a land lying open and prostrate under the heat of a punishing sun.

The fat manager had been right. This was no corridor-walker.

So why then, all of a sudden, was my scar itching?

I kept my hand away from my head and looked around for the transhaus manager but he did not seem to be in the room.

"Yes," I said. "I'm Pike."

"Good," she said and smiled. "Could we go somewhere . . . and talk?"

Normally, I could expect the fat manager to be here in his office to give me the receipted bill for my sleep-time. But just because he wasn't now in the room did not mean that he

15

couldn't be somewhere outside it with a thick ear pressed close against a thin part of the wall. And if she had something to say that she was in some way not sure of . . . ?

This is where I should have cut out, the way the scar on my head was acting up. But I pressed it hard with my palm, faking the scratching. Don't be silly, I said to myself, and maybe to my scar. If this is the kind of a package they're putting trouble up in these days, where do I line up for my share?

But aloud I said, "I'm . . . I'm just on my way out for something to eat. Would you join me, Miss . . . ?"

But she let my question just hang there unanswered. She looked at her wrist-chrono, pushing back the broad bangle with a fingertip.

"Thank you," she said. "But I don't think we have the time. Couldn't . . . couldn't we just talk as we walked?"

I shrugged. If she didn't want to be overheard, then just being outside and in motion was no particular help against anyone even half serious about listening in on what she had to say. But then, maybe on her world they didn't have directional pickups and tracking equipment.

"Fine," I said. "That will be just fine," and I stepped back for her to go out the door before me.

She did, but as she passed the manager's desk coming toward me, I saw her lay two coins on its flat top; heard their dull, plastic click.

Two coins. Double eagles. Forty Earth dollars just for finding a photographer among the registration slips in his "occupied" file? Who needed an itching scar to set his teeth on edge?

All the same I followed her out of the slowly revolving main door and onto the spaceport perimeter walk.

CHAPTER THREE

Transit worlds, I was beginning to suspect, came in but two varieties. Cold enough to freeze the proverbial nut off its bolt, or hot enough to fry.

Poldrogi was the frying kind, bearable only because of the extreme shortness of its day. It was little more than a place in space where a freighter could warp out long enough to make the planetfall necessary to transship a cargo or to drop off, amid a general shaking of heads, a diehard passenger or two bound for one of the rim worlds.

After all, a man did not head for what the planets closer to the galaxy nucleus called "the home of the loon and the loner" unless he was pretty much one or the other himself, and the rim-worlders were becoming, more or less, a breed unto themselves.

It had seemed to me to be a better place than most to look for the unusual and the unexpected.

The unusual and the unexpected.

Like the booted and fur-bangled figure of the girl walking ahead of me. Her home planet must be a scorching place for her to walk so lightly in the heavy press of *Poldrogi's* heat.

I blinked against the glare of the high sun, my eyes watering, and moved to overtake her, but she had stopped by the side of a small, dark-green-and-black surface skimmer and was motioning me to slide into its small double seat.

I hesitated, my head scar itching, and she chose to misinterpret my hanging back.

"I'm sorry," she said. "But the hostel had no cars with aircooled interiors."

That shouldn't have surprised her and maybe it didn't. When you were an out-of-the-way place like *Poldrogi*, you had to ship in just about everything you used, and that included a small surface skimmer.

And if you wanted it to reach you in something that resembled a usable lifetime, then you had to span the distance from planet to planet, from star to star, at a rate a great deal better than the speed of light.

17

That meant the space warp.

That also meant heavy power expenditure even though the warp didn't seem to go by how physically large an object was, nor by how great the distance you wanted to send it. It seemed to be the breaking into and the breaking out of the force field that ate up all that power.

And that seemed to be a function of the object's mass; its pure weight. A tiny shotgun pellet, for example, needed no more power to be sent to a distant sporting world than did an inflated target marker, if they both weighed the same.

And power, as always, costed.

This didn't mean that the traffic was light; far from it. But it did mean that if your hostel was a cut less than fashionable, you didn't waste your money bringing in something with the weight of a car-cooling unit just in case one of your transients mightn't be willing to take a little of the heat you lived with.

One thing, though, that the weight-power property of the warp made cheap was the galactic mail.

Half a planet's daily communications could be, and were, made to fit onto a tissue-thin rectangle of plastic about the size of a man's palm and weighing next to nothing. Flat, automatically guided, web containers, weighing as little as the numberless electronically recorded messages packed into them, streamed into and out of asteroid and satellite postal substations.

But straight mail was the only kind of service available at low price. To make a parcel of my camera invited arm-and-leg shipping rates. Yet even a thick sheaf of the holograms that represented the pictures I'd taken with it could be sent anywhere in the galaxy, as a pinpoint-sized pattern of magnetic impulses, for literally the price of a single stamp. And, of course, infinitely faster than any light or radio wave could have carried them.

I shook my head at the girl holding open the skimmer door.

"I'd like to know a little of what you have in mind," I said to her. "After all, I have my license to think of."

This was true, but only partly. How could I tell her that my scar was itching me to the point where the sweat I felt trickling down my sides inside my jumpsuit wasn't all due to *Poldrogi's* heat?

She looked puzzled. "Your license? To take a picture?"

"No," I said. "I don't need a license to take a picture. I mean my license to carry a camera."

18

How far out was her native world for her not to know that, since the hard lesson of the Second Peace Action, cameras, recorders, transmitters, anything larger than the personal, limited-range receivers most people carried, had to be specially licensed? And the licenses, issued by BuPersSec, the Bureau of Personnel Security, were almost impossible to get without a Service record to prove your dependability.

Still, the galaxy *was* some hundred thousand lightyears across, and she might really not have heard of a CE license.

Or, more to the point, like most people who knew that a camera would record whatever they put in front of it, she still just didn't think of one as being a piece of communications equipment.

But fine wrist bones or no, a transit world was no place for a photographer to be hung up without a license that was a must if he was to ply his trade.

Not that the *Poldrogi* police could lift mine from me permanently. BuPersSec had not left *that* potential blackjack to the discretion of any local satrap. But the police of any planet could impound a man's CE license pending an investigation and a hearing before the Bureau.

And if I'd had the money credits to risk being stranded on a transit world for even a short time without the use of my cameras, I'd be doing my sleeping in a place other than a spaceport transhaus.

Poldrogi was no different from any place that existed chiefly by catering to people who just passed through it. There is action, there is a ready flow of money credits. But the flow is in the main from transient to local.

And if you happen to be a transient with the bad luck, or the bad judgment, to go broke. . . . Well, who can blame the local if he takes it out on you for the slights, the insults, the downright indignities and indecencies he's had to put up with from transients with more money and better brains than to get themselves stranded on his world.

The look on the girl's face was still one of puzzlement, but she'd been holding it too long. She may not have known about a CE license, but she was stalling about something. Something that had brought her to the spaceport transhaus, and which she now looked to be groping around for a way to start to talk about.

The spaceport transhaus.

The *Poldrogi* spaceport transhaus.

I slid into the skimmer seat. "Let's go," I said, and added, to myself, "before my brains catch up with my head."

CHAPTER FOUR

She drove the skimmer well, and her handling of it, her giving it no more acceleration than it needed to clear the spaceport tarmac, her not wasting its fuel on a jackrabbit start, all gave clear indication that she was accustomed to travel in power-starved areas.

"Look, Miss. . . ," I said, letting my voice hang in the air once more.

This time she finished for me.

"Mrs.," she said. "Mrs. Brigit Plagiar. My husband is Anton Plagiar. You have heard of him, perhaps?"

Anton Plagiar. I played the name over in my head, but it rang no bells.

But the Mrs., and her seeming not to know how to begin with her proposition did.

A transom job.

Back at her hostel her husband was in a room with somebody he shouldn't have been with . . . or she knew when he would be. And she wanted my camera and me poking our snout through the transom above the locked door. My laser and its reference beam would flood the room with their thin ruby light when they went off, but once I had the evidence, that didn't really matter.

A transom job.

I would have bet on it.

I would have lost.

At the first service intersection she turned her skimmer, not to the right and the hostels and transient traps as I'd expected her to do, but to the left.

To the left and toward the residential area of the spaceport complex.

Toward the sun-bleached wood-and-baked-mud residential area and through it. Through it and out into the open country beyond, the air cushion of the skimmer sending up a low billow of dust and small stones from the parched surface of the raw, unpaved road. The rush of air past the open windows, though hot, was more bearable than standing still.

20

As we rode between the sparse and stunted growth, she talked against the wind in what must have been, for her, an unaccustomed shout. And as she did, I wondered why my blasted scar would not stop its itching.

This was no transom job for it to fret over. Far from it.

Anton Plagiar, her husband, was a man with a big bank-roll and a bigger heart.

For this I had to take her word although, being his wife, she should certainly be the one to know. But then I suppose a man doesn't top his money gifts by taking the trouble to become a competent magician for the sole purpose of going from planet to planet, from health home to health home, putting on shows for their shut-ins, without there being something in his heart other than the blood it had to pump.

They were newly arrived on *Poldrogi* she was telling me, Anton and Brigit Plagiar, but already he was planning to give a demonstration of magic for the children at the Wayfarer's Home which, incidentally, we ought to be coming into sight of soon.

Could I ... would I photograph his performance so that she, Brigit, could add the pictures to her scrapbook?

That sounded innocent enough, so why did she seem to be having so much trouble getting the words out?

But scrapbook pictures. My financial spirits sagged. That meant that simple blowups from my record camera would do, and not the 3D shots I'd hoped her job would call for.

But no. Holograms and their three-dimensional reconstructions were what she wanted. And the way she began pulling credits from her shoulder purse when we got to the question of my fee, sure made it seem that their cost didn't seem to be much of a handicap to her, although I couldn't help but notice the last little groping motion her hand made in her bag before it finally came out empty.

All the ready cash she had for some scrapbook pictures?

But I nodded. "It's a deal," I said, hoping she wouldn't think I was some kind of a nut from the way I was rubbing my palm on my itching scar.

Poldrogi's fast-moving sun was past its peak, but a full press of heat burned down on us still when Brigit coasted her skimmer to a stop and we lost the breeze of our motion.

A woven-reed fence, shoulder high, and through its broad opened gates, a scrubby lawn hip deep in children, all yelling and shouting. And beyond them the flat, one-story baked-mud-brick building of the Home itself.

Bushes, dry and stunted looking, cluttered the area close

up to the Home and were scattered in clumps about the crowded lawn, their only effect being to emphasize the burned-out look of the place.

Twilight couldn't come any too soon on a world like this.

In the middle of the alleged lawn and all the furor, there floated, about a yard-and-a-half off the ground, a circular platform, and when I saw it I nodded my approval.

Long ago, when I was only a little bigger than these children noisily swarming all around Brigit and me, magic had been a pretty serious interest with me, and it pleased me to see the mark of a man who knew what he was about. There is nothing like open space under a performer's stage to put things like trapdoors or hidden assistants out of his audience's mind.

I felt a hand lightly on my arm and looked down to see Brigit smiling up at me. She said something, but I couldn't make it out in all that youthful din. I held up a hand, found a small pebble at my feet, and tossed it under the floating platform.

To hold a stage up off the ground with ordinary hover units was, of course, out of the question the way their blast churned up the dust and debris and everything else in their path. But you could use the new miniaturized anti-grav units, or you could just let the stage sit on posts and a solid base and mask the view with the crisscrossing rays of dozens of tiny refraction units.

Either way the units not only cost the proverbial satchelful of credits, but took a high degree of technical competance to set up.

The arcing path of the pebble I'd thrown glowed faintly blue for a brief moment and I knew that Plagiar was using anti-grav units and that his under-platform space was really empty of hiding places.

"You are a man of no small curiosity," Brigit laughed when we were free of the press of the midget crowd and I could hear her. And on her the tiny moustache of sweat beading her upper lip looked good.

Nosy would have been a better word for her to have used, but I didn't correct her. I'd just noticed, at the X-braced wood door of the pressed-down-looking main building, a cluster of three or four men in ordinary blue-and-yellow business tunics. Compactly built, they looked to be, all young, all tough looking.

And they seemed to suddenly be very interested in me.

In me, or in me and Brigit hanging from my arm.

I must have hesitated in my stride, because I felt Brigit's hand on my arm give it a little tug and she led me right up the single broad step flanked by the scrubby plantings and toward the eyeing group.

Philanthropist her husband might be, and here to give a few moments of pleasure to some unfortunate children, but I knew a phalanx of bodyguards from a group of ordinary plainclothes police when I saw one and, for that matter, so did my scar. But with Brigit on my right arm and my camera off its strap around my neck and in my left hand, there wasn't much I could do but let it itch.

We went up to and past the squat phalanx, they tracking us with their heads and eyes as we moved.

At the last possible moment, one of them leaned forward and I braced myself, for what I didn't really know, but he only hooked a thick finger over the outside latch of the door and pulled it open for us.

"Thank you," I said, and when I looked back over my shoulder for the answer I did not hear him give, a strangeness in the look of the closing door nudged at my consciousness.

A strangeness that made it all the way and brought me up to turn and stare to be sure that I'd seen aright.

I had.

In this strange place, the inside of the front door seemed to have no knob ... nor any other way of opening it that I could see.

CHAPTER FIVE

Hard was not the word to describe the look of Anton Plagiar's face. Driving was not it either. Yet I had the feeling of looking at a man who was capable of exerting great pressure if it moved him to do so.

Inside, I shrugged. A man did not get to have the financial stature he appeared to have without having some look of tautness about him. Or maybe it was just the natural and to-be-expected keying up of a performer before he goes into his act. After all, Brigit *had* told me that they'd more-or-less just arrived on *Poldrogi* and already he was about to perform for its children.

Physically, Anton Plagiar was a small man with thick white hair built high on his head, and a thin white moustache to go with it. He looked to be as compactly put together as one of his own bodyguards, the way, I was beginning to notice, the rim-world people seemed in the main to be. But then I suppose they couldn't help but grow that way in a place where livable space and food were anything but easy to come by.

But Plagiar looked a bit old for that to have been the case with him, although, after seeing Brigit, I may just have expected him to be a much younger man.

But the standard electric-blue evening tights and short silver jacket he wore had never come from the shop of any rim-world tailor. "Sleek nucleus," their cut spelled, and I would have bet that no provincial tailor had ever gotten his hands on material that could drape like that in his life.

Brigit did not introduce us, nor, for that matter, did Plagiar even so much as nod in her direction when we came from the stuffy entry into the not much airier main hall.

In his place, I think I would have done something more than casually slide my eyes across my wife, particularly if she came in hanging on an arm the way Brigit suddenly seemed to be hanging on mine. Although I suppose I should have been happy that Plagiar didn't seem to mind any more than he did because, now that I was well inside the room I saw

24

that there were other young men scattered around it, all conservatively dressed in blue-and-yellow, until the ordinary business tunics began to look to me like some kind of unobtrusive uniform.

But Brigit had slid open the door to what looked like a small study and was taking my camera from my hand. I didn't want to let it go, but I supposed that with all of the bully boys that seemed to be thronging the place, it would be more than well guarded on the small table beside Brigit's shoulder purse.

"A small drink," she said, "while we wait." And sure enough, looking past her into the shaded chamber, I saw, on a low table in front of the divan, glasses and a tall, cool-looking bottle that made my mouth water just to look at it.

But I never got to find out what its contents tasted like because it seemed that no sooner had Brigit got me settled on the divan and was starting to fuss with the glasses, when the door she'd slid closed behind her opened and a bully boy stuck in his head.

He spoke with the same strange accent I'd noticed on Brigit, but heavier by far. But his message was plain enough.

The master wanted me on stage and ready when he made his entrance, and that was right now.

I sighed, disentangled my long legs from each other and those of the divan table, and followed the bully boy. Half-absently I noticed, when I scooped up my camera, that it felt vaguely strange in my hand. I glanced at it, but there was no mistaking its larger-than-standard size, the special pic-hold finder. It was my camera all right.

There was a flurry of activity going on in the main hall as I passed through it. Two of the bully boys had long red capes over their shoulders, the hoods thrown back. One of them was fiddling with a glowing, lilac "A" on the tip of one finger; the other had already pasted his over his left eyebrow and was patting it more firmly in place with a stubby middle finger.

I grinned to myself. Androids. There was a law in the galaxy, heavily enforced, that an android had to wear his telltale badge, fitted to him when he was made, so that a human would not be deceived by a resemblance that, with high-grade work, was often impossible to detect by the unaided eye or touch.

But there was no law on any planet that a man couldn't masquerade as an android, and Plagiar wouldn't be the first

25

magician to outfit his assistants to look like something more glamorous than simple humans.

And right now, because of their rarity and high cost, androids were both glamorous and objects of great curiosity. One would have been a rarity. Two, on the same stage with him, would give Plagiar's act a decided fillip.

Plagiar, himself, was busy fitting the loose hood of the red cloak he too had donned over his white hair and down to shield his face.

My grin broadened when I saw that. Three men, all looking the same, I was sure, would follow me out to the floating platform.

"Do not begin until I give you a signal." It was Brigit, who had come out of the small study and now seemed to be headed for the back of the building.

I nodded, smiling. I was pretty sure I knew what Plagiar's opening effect was going to be.

At the blank front door the bully boy stopped and rapped on its heavy panel. It was opened for him, in a moment, by one of the bully boys outside.

Is there no way out of this place from the inside?

"There," said the bully boy guilding me, pointing at the circular stage poised in the air at the center of the lawn and the mass of waiting children. "You go, and you wait."

I went, and I was ready to wait.

CHAPTER SIX

A yard-and-a-half off the ground. Plagiar's performing stage floated about chest high to me and now that I'd pressed through the steaming, chattering mass of children that circled it and was close to it, I saw that it was revolving very slowly, giving the spiral pattern in magenta and yellow on its floor an almost hypnotic quality to watch.

I shook my head, blinked my eyes. That took care of anyone seeing a trapdoor or any other kind of opening in the stage floor.

I leaned down to look under the platform, steadying myself with one hand on its edge as I did so.

Firm.

The platform was not only firm, but my hand felt as though there was a hidden pressure pushing against its weight.

Gyros.

Plagiar's platform not only had anit-grav units to hold it up, but an internal system of gyroscopes to keep it steady against the notoriously bouncy feel of shifting weight pressures. He must have a potful of money or the men working for him were technical geniuses ... maybe both. Yet, I'd never heard of him.

The platform was thin at its edge, no more than four inches, I guessed. But it thickened in toward its center, so gradually that the foot or so depth it had at that point was difficult to see even when you knew it had to be there and were looking for it as I was.

Wait. The man had said to wait.

I looked around for Brigit, wanting to locate her now so that I'd know where to look for her signal to start shooting when her husband came on stage.

I couldn't find her. And then, out of the corner of my eye, I saw a motion at the top of the Home building. It was Brigit, waving to me. She was at a corner of the roof, behind a waist-high parapet. It was a logical enough place from which to watch her husband's performance, even though it did mean she would be out in the raw heat of the sun.

But then, even with the bushes, there was no more real shade down here than there was up there, and the roof at least had the illusion of airiness.

I waved back to her and then saw that her motion was really a signal. She wanted me up on the stage?

I pointed to myself and to the stage and saw her nod.

I'd covered many shows, presentations, speeches, but always from the audience level or unobtrusively from the wings. No performer I'd ever met had wanted a photographer onstage during his act, diverting the audience's attention away from him.

But she was Plagiar's wife and she should certainly know how he wanted himself covered.

I shrugged, set my camera on the platform, noting once again its strange feel, and clambered up after it.

There was a blare of trumpets, from where I could not tell, and then I found the sound was coming from under my feet. Speakers, in the platform, of course.

The babble of the children stopped for a moment, and then there was a shout of anticipation from their treble voices.

I turned and saw three red-cloaked figures, their long garb trailing the ground, seemingly floating toward us.

They circled the platform once, twice, then vaulted lightly onto it and dropped down at once to become three brooding, hooded figures hunched at equal distances along its perimeter. None of them had come anywhere close to the center of the platform.

I looked at it now, my eyes squinting down, guarding against what I knew had to come.

From under my feet, a crescendo of sound and then the flash. The flash of bright light and the billow of colorful smoke and, in its midst, arms spread wide, the white-haired, moustached figure in electric-blue and silver.

I did not need to look at Brigit to know that there was no point in photographing this sudden apparition. It looked like Anton Plagiar, it was supposed to, but it wasn't Anton Plagiar.

This was the man who had borne the heat and discomfort of being penned up in the compartment hidden in the platform's foot-thick center since it had been first set up, perhaps hours earlier. It was a centuries-old technique for a magical appearance, and the gasp it brought from the audience of

28

children showed that it was still as good as it had ever been.

And now the tempo of the music coming from the platform's hidden speakers picked up. The three red-hooded figures rose and began to glide along the edge of the platform with their peculiar flowing gait.

Gliding and circling, raising and lowering their bodies; swifter and swifter grew their pace, tighter and tighter their circling path, passing first on one side of me and then on the other.

And the Anton-double was waving his arms and then, suddenly, to the accompaniment of another gasp of children's voices, in each of his hands was a streaming banner of yellow-and-magenta to match the spiral of the platform floor.

About his head and body he waved them; their streamers trailing and spiraling, the red figures gliding and circling.

Into the air he threw them. Straight up and with a mighty heave.

High they rose. Higher and higher and with all eyes following their soaring path.

Mine included.

And then I caught myself and snapped my eyes back to the center of the stage where the three red figures, their cloaks billowing, had converged upon and were swirling about the one electric-blue-and-silver clad one.

And I knew that when the soaring banners fell back to the stage the Anton-double would be inside one of the hooded cloaks and the man who stepped forward to catch them and go on with the show would be the real Anton Plagiar.

I brought my camera up to the ready, to catch the first of my pictures as he did so.

I brought my camera up and the strangeness of its feel in my hands almost forced its way into the forefront of my consciousness.

Almost, but not quite. Yet, just as a craftsman can pick up a tool from a benchful of others looking exactly like it and know it to be his own, so my hands felt in my camera a strangeness as I lifted it up to my face.

On the rim of my vision I saw a movement and looking, saw Brigit waving, frantically it seemed to me, from her vantage point on the roof.

I looked with my eyes and my mind, but my hands moved on their own in a pattern set by long habit.

Down they pointed the camera and they squeezed its release.

Once, they squeezed it to check its operation against the strangeness of the heft they sensed. Downward, to keep the flash of even my low-intensity and relatively safe laser light from striking needlessly the eyes of my subject.

Once, they squeezed, and I was staggered.

Under my feet the platform shuddered and dipped and, whirring through the space my head had just dropped away from, was a sound I hadn't heard since the Second Peace Action.

I heard the thin, almost inaudible passage of the masher beam from a sniper's weapon. Had it even so much as brushed my skull, the bone-conducted vibrations would have homogenized my brain and I would have been dead even before my body could begin to fall.

But even with the near-miss, my head hummed with the passage of its peripheral shock wave and my reflexes were numbed to the point where I could not fully control my body.

But numbed reflexes or no, my body remembered its combat-learned lessons for itself and started to drop me flat to the floor of the now tilting and lurching stage.

As I went down I saw, following the pointing of my camera in my hands, still nosed downward, a snaking, living gash forming itself in the garish pattern of the platform floor.

In a flash of understanding as brilliant as only hindsight can be, I knew the reason for the feel of strangeness my camera had.

Someone, and he could have had the chance only while my camera was resting on the small table beside Brigit's purse, had removed the heart unit from my relatively safe photographic laser and slipped into its clip a focused, high-intensity, killer unit.

This was not a particularly startling devising. After all, hadn't the original laser used for its light source a photographic flashtube?

But killer units operated in microsecond bursts of infrared light. *This* beam was continuous and, squeeze my release as hard as my masher-beam-stunned reflexes would let me, *I couldn't shut it off.*

And *that* was startling. A man who could build a high-intensity, sustained-energy exciter and its power supply, and do it compactly enough to add almost undetectable ounces to the weight of my camera, had a degree of simple technical competence, that, if nothing else, bordered on the near-miraculous.

And I sincerely did not know if I marveled more at this than I did at his, or their, audacity in using so hoary a dodge as hiding a weapon in a camera; a dodge that, except for my hands' own animal sense in detecting the strange feel of the camera they held, might have worked, perhaps because of its very hoariness.

The slashing, snaking laser, from the platform's mad pitching and rolling, must be playing havoc with the anti-grav units holding it up, the gyros trying to keep it level.

And now I consciously fought my own beam-weakened hands to keep the camera from slipping out of their grip. Fought to hold it and to keep it pointed downward and away from the now roiling, screaming mass of children around me.

Fighting the laser beam, and swearing at the animals who, to kill a man, would choose a time and a weapon that, like a hose that could not be turned off, would spray its death at the youngsters pressing close around him.

CHAPTER SEVEN

I hit the ground rolling, flung there partly by the pitching and tilting of the platform, partly by my own badly coordinated efforts to escape.

Over and around me was now the obscene-sounding blat of a police stun-gun firing; the Home's own guard, perhaps. I felt a sudden wetness on my ear and neck but I did not reach up my hand to see if I had been hit.

My camera was under me; I'd managed that in my falling. Flat, pointing downward, let its hellish laser bore the ground.

The children, at least, were safe from it and whoever came to retrieve it should, after what had happened, have enough sense to approach it with caution.

I could not run; my stunned nerves would not direct my legs to a proper rising sequence.

I rolled. Like a giant, elongated tumbleweed before a hot wind of panic, I rolled. Rolled for the shelter of the scrawny bushes pressing against the base of the Home building.

It saved me. That, and the masking roil of screaming children.

Rolling, I was flat to the ground and I suppose they expected to see the running figure I'd tried to be except that my knees wouldn't life me.

A running figure . . . and one going *away* from the area.

I rolled toward its center, thinking not of the guards or the crowd, but of the sniper. From the direction of the house he'd fired, and only the one time. High, he seemed to be, and my instinct was to get in under his gun, below his line of fire.

Into the bushes I rolled, snaking between them and the dusty wall of the building.

I lay panting, shaking my head although I knew that it would be no help in clearing it of the shockwave-induced hum.

I had never before been hit by the shock wave that traveled, like a hard, invisible funnel, on the periphery of a

32

masher beam. And, from the feel of it, this one time was enough for me.

Experimentally, I flexed my fingers. Their strength did not seem to be merely diminished, but also came and went, came and went, like the phasing of a sound wave.

There was a weakness ... and then a slow building to what seemed like normal strength ... and then the weakness ... and the strengthening again.

My hearing ... my vision ... both seemed to ebb and flow ... ebb and flow ... following the same unsettling pattern.

I peered as best as I could up the low front of the building, looking for the sniper.

Leaning over the parapet, scanning the bushes that half-hid me, was Brigit. Then, at least, the sniper hadn't been on the roof, else she would have seen him.

But maybe he was, and maybe she had. Was she with me or had she set me up to kill her husband, then be knocked off myself before I could defend or explain myself? Explain myself, with the transhaus manager to back at least that part of my story, that it was she who had sought me out, and that I'd never even seen her husband before now, much less had a motive to murder him.

But what if she were as innocent of intent to kill as I; wasn't another young wife with a sniper boyfriend and an urge to nudge an aging husband out of the triangle?

She could clear me ... and completely.

The sky behind Brigit had grown less eyeball-searing. *Poldrogi's* quick sun was not yet low but it was getting there. I peered up at her as best as my phasing eyes and the thin bramble-branches would let me.

The killer laser.

There was the killer laser in my camera. Had she provided the opportunity for it to be installed on purpose?

She needn't have. You could build the laser then, knowing of Brigit's propensity for having her husband photographed for her scrapbook, just wait for the opportunity to insert it into some unsuspecting photographer's camera. It could just have happened to be me. It *had* happened to be me.

Men and women were mingled with the quieting children now, leading some out and away through the open gate, herding the rest toward the Home, and toward me, hidden in the sparse growth at the base of its facade.

And there were those of the new arrivals who stood or ran, shouting, still seeking me, still circling the grounds; the now sagged-to-the-ground platform.

Plagiar was not in sight, nor were his bully boys.

Brigit. Dare I risk showing myself to her, hoping that she could make it down to me to intercede for me . . . to explain?

Or, if I did, would she shout and point me out to those who were hunting me and let the mob perhaps do for her what the sniper's beam hadn't been able to?

I peered up at her leaning out over the parapet and mentally I flipped a coin again and again. Dare I trust her, or dare I not?

And then I laughed and the mental coin stood on its edge. There was no need for me to risk my life on a wrong decision. All I had to do was to wait until I could hear what story she told the police I knew must respond, if they weren't already on the way, to the crowd's clamor.

If she cleared me I could emerge from hiding. If she had her own tale to tell . . . at least I'd know where I stood in *that* quarter.

Hide, until I could hear a newscast or see a newsfax.

Hide, but not here. The cover was thin and the police would search the grounds as a matter of routine.

Get away, but how?

On moonless *Poldrogi,* with its short, short day, night fell almost as rapidly as pulling down a shade, but I could not wait for its cover.

I could not wait, period.

Among the men gathering on the Home lawn were those who wore jumpsuits and coveralls not unlike the one I had on. Perhaps if I emerged and moved about purposefully, pretended to be one of them, looking for myself? After all, how many of them had been here to see me on the platform and so could recognize me now? Very few, if any at all, now that Plagiar and his bully boys had vanished.

And to be caught in the act of hiding would, in itself, be a damning identification.

I had no real choice but to try to brazen it out. It was either that or take to my heels in headlong flight, and, by this action, betray myself to the gathering crowd.

I waited for a rising phase in the unnerving ebb and flow, ebb and flow of my strength and when it came, took a deep, wavering breath, raised myself up . . . and stepped as casually as I could out of the shadow of the bushes and onto the lawn.

A shout, a pointing . . . and an animal surge of the crowd in my direction.

But I had seen it for myself and was already running.

Running as only the desperate can run.

Running for the all-encompassing fence. Running and praying that the strength of my legs, my body, my hands, would not fail me, abandon me to the thing that was finding its throat behind me.

My neck, my shoulder, the side of my head. The feeling of wetness I'd felt strike at them. The stun-gun. Its charge had not hit me, but its projectile had been from a riot shell.

A riot shell, designed not only to stun the man it struck, but to spray and splash his companions around him with a telltale dye so that for forty-eight hours, at least, no matter how they ran, how they tried to blend with the innocents about them, they could not conceal from a seeking eye the guilty fact of their presence on the scene.

My shoulder, my neck, my head ... they glowed in the lowering angle of the sun with a green so vivid it was almost audible.

I am not an athlete, I have never been, but my urgency lifted me over the fence and into the scrubby brush beyond it.

I ran. Swearing at the brambles that would catch and hold me back. Swearing at the assassin who would make of me a tool. Swearing most of all at myself for not heeding the warning of my scar when first I set eyes on Brigit ... first heard her speak to me in her oddly accented voice.

I ran, dodging, falling, changing my direction, hearing the sounds of pursuit grow and diminish and sweating out the nerve-stretching strain of not knowing if they were really falling behind me or if it was just my own flawed hearing playing me false.

I ran, evading yet never losing my pursuers, until I stumbled, in the at-last-fallen darkness, into the black and weed-dotted waters of a *Poldrogi* lake.

CHAPTER EIGHT

I sat, over my head in black water, breathing through a reed, feeling the ooze of the lakebottom beneath me sucking at me; feeling the unsettling bump and nudge of night-blinded things slithering against me.

I sat, waiting for those who would make of me their prey to tire in their hunt.

Tire, not enough to abandon their searching for me, I could not hope for that. To them, I was a would-be killer, and vicious.

Vicious and callous, to place their children in so terrible a danger. Their determination to seize me was, I was certain, as great as mine would have been had I been in their place; had it been a child of mine so placed in jeopardy.

But they would tire enough, I hoped, to be for the moment satisfied with the setting up of a guard and the waiting out of the night that, on their moonless planet, was shorter, even, than the time of their daylight.

A letting up of vigilance that might give me the slim edge I needed to evade them completely, or at least until the telltale dye lost its green glow . . . or I could learn how Brigit meant to tell her story.

Around me, the water churned up by the blast from the crossing and recrossing hover-craft had let up its tugging at me. They might still be aloft, their heat-detectors dangling, but if they were, they had at least shifted their operations away from the weeds in which I was hiding.

Cautiously, I raised myself up, rocking a little to break the sucking grip of the mud that would hold me, until my head was clear enough of the water's surface for me to listen.

From across the lake came the sound of the hover-craft beating.

Good. For that much, then, I could be thankful. They were now searching to find me on the far shore which I probably would have struck out for had I been able to swim.

But I couldn't swim, so I was still on the same side of the

lake as when I'd plunged into it. A hard fact I was hoping my pursuers would not guess.

Slowly, keeping my ear on the high sound of raised voices as best as my phasing hearing would let me, and using it as a guide, I groped along the lake bottom with feet I could not fully trust to have the strength to hold me, the full sense of feel to guide me.

Breathing through my reed where the water was so deep as to close over my head; slithering on my stomach and hands where it wasn't, I made my way along the shore, expecting at any moment to hear a rousing shout of discovery, feel the stupefying blast of a stun-gun, or the knifing slash of a pistol's laser.

And at long last, the voices in my ear were faint, even when my hearing reached a high point in its ebb and flow, ebb and flow.

In toward the shore I turned. In toward the faintly blacker mass the scrubby undergrowth made against the starshine that was the only relief from its darkness that *Poldrogi's* moonless night afforded.

In I moved, until the upward slope of the rock-studded bank was unmistakable, the water frothing lightly against my ankles.

Up the bank I staggered, fell forward onto it with something akin to a gasp of relief, in spite of its sharp and craggy feel.

I did not hear him approach. In the blackness I certainly did not see him.

Face down, I felt only the hard pressure of his weapon on the back of my skull; heard only his voice, flat and quiet in my ear.

"Freeze," he said.

I froze.

CHAPTER NINE

"Piot Kval," the man behind the battered wood desk said in his heavy *Poldrogi* accent.

His uniform tunic was open at the neck and mottled to a dark brown with sweat. In his hand he held a self-contained power fan larger than any I'd seen before, and he was making no progress at all with it on the sweat that beaded his red face and bald head. If he'd used a mirror instead, his eyes would have put a frost line wherever they touched.

I stared at him.

Stared at him and at my camera on the desk top in front of him.

My camera. Clean and undamaged and looking as though I'd never crushed it to the earth beneath my body; as though it had never held any laser but the one in its own innocuous speedlight.

"Piot Kval," he repeated and waited for my answer.

I shook my head. "I don't know the name," I said. And I didn't.

"You do not know the name," he said. He reached out to his desk, picked up my wallet from the small array of my possessions spread out beside my camera; a scattering of keys, coins, pocket flotsam, my sleeve camera, kept safe from the cold *Poldrogi* lake by its waterproof casing.

Slowly, almost lazily, using only his one hand, his other not putting down his fan, he examined his prize, fingering the few plastic credits in their separate compartment, idly turning over the leaves of the card section.

Without saying a word, he was putting a chill in the air.

I pulled closer about me the thin blanket the police had given me while they went over my sodden jumpsuit and boots. It reeked of disinfectant, but it was better than standing before the police corporal in nothing but my skin. My head and neck still glowed a bright green, I knew. They had done nothing about the riot marker dye I was stained with. My beam-shocked strength came and went. I fought myself to keep it from showing.

I knew what the cold-eyed corporal was looking for, and I

was sure that he knew I knew. Yet when he came to it he flicked right on past it and, if he wanted my heart to skip a beat, it did.

He flicked the small panel over, then flicked it back, as though he'd just that moment noticed its contents.

He pressed open the clear plastic envelope shape, inserted a heavy thumb, sat there, not pulling out the yellow plastic rectangle, not taking his thumb from it.

He looked up at me. "You gave us a great deal of trouble, you know," he said. "It was all my men could do to keep our people from overtaking you."

If he meant to sweat me, he was doing it. I couldn't help licking my lips. "Thank you," I said, and I think I might have meant it.

I couldn't take my eyes off his thumb on my Communications Equipment license.

Ebb and flow went my strength. Ebb and flow.

"There are no thanks required," he said, speaking in the same matter-of-fact manner as had the fat transhaus manager when he'd turned aside my thanks for calling me to what I'd thought was a photo assignment. "If we had tried to save you from them openly, our people might have resisted our efforts and it would have caused an embarrassment all around. It is better that they should believe for a while that they lost you of themselves."

He ran his thumb back and forth over the face of my CE license. If he meant to remind me that he could pull it, he didn't have to. "Would it make a difference if I told you your fingerprint had not yet been obliterated from the record?" he said.

I didn't follow him. I didn't follow anything. My camera, battered, perhaps even damaged where someone had smashed it open to get at its killer laser, would have been a starting point for me to at least begin to tell my story.

My camera, clean and pristine looking, on the corporal's desk. What could I say that it didn't give the lie to before I opened my mouth?

I was staring at it and now I saw the corporal eyeing it with a flicker of interest.

"Look," I said, taking the plunge. "Am I being charged with anything specific?"

The corporal's eyebrows went up. "Specific? A charge?" He smiled, but his eyes did not warm, and neither did he take his thumb from my CE license. "You feel a guilt, perhaps? You must remember that you ran?"

"I ran," I said. "I heard a masher beam, I got sprayed with riot dye, and the mob took off after me. I ran. I ran as hard as I could."

I did not mention that my head had not let up its humming since the near-miss passage of the beam, nor that the phasing in and out of my strength was just on the rim of my control. I did not mention this because what I wanted was out, and not to be held for even medical observation.

But if the corporal did not finish with me soon, I knew the wavelike surging would slip from my control and be as evident to him, and anyone else within spraying distance, as would be the effect of any wavelike, surging action on any tired and queasy stomach.

"A masher beam," the corporal was saying. "You are familiar with the sound of a sniper's weapon?"

"Look among my cards in your hand," I said. "You'll find my SpaceNav discharge. I'm familiar with the sound of a sniper's weapon."

"Yes. And yet is it not most curious? A weapon capable of firing a masher beam ... at a children's home? You could not have been mistaken about the sound? A flying insect perhaps? Coming at a critical moment?"

His thumb did not move from my CE license. And from his tone I couldn't tell if I was the only one to have heard the beam ... or if he even believed what I'd said.

Believe what I said? He had the look of a man you'd just taken a big pot from asking to see your openers.

I touched a hand to the dye on my head. "This is no mistake. It set me up for the crowd. And something was going on to get them riled up."

He was silent a long moment, the only sound in the room being that of my own breath in my nostrils and the faint whir of his fan.

Abruptly he pulled his thumb clear of my CE license, spread my wallet on the desk top in front of him. "These," he said, jabbing at my license with a thick forefinger. "These they do not hand out without some discretion. The fact that you are the possessor of an authentic one ..."

An authentic one! Then the corporal had checked it out more thoroughly than his casual manner with it had indicated.

". . . possessor of an authentic one would indicate that you are a man of some dependability."

He folded over my wallet, leaned back in his chair. "Mr. Pike," he said, "I can tell you that the dye on your head was

40

not fired at you by any of my men. It could be a . . . a joke of practicality, or it could be that someone has designs upon you.

He eyed me a moment. "It could also be that you have not wished to confide in me . . . that you are involved in something you do not wish to speak of to the police. . . ."

He let his voice trail off and when, after a long moment I did not speak, he raised it. "Kuba," he called, and, when a sweating police private came in through the door behind me, "please see to it that the dye on Mr. Pike's head is counteracted and that his things are returned to him."

He was no longer looking at me and his voice sounded disinterested. Was he turning me loose? It sounded like it.

The police private saluted. "Yes, Corporal," he said, and took hold of my arm.

I pointed at my camera and my things on the desk. "Could I take them with me now?" I asked.

"If you wish," the corporal said. "Kuba will have a receipt for you to sign."

When I hefted my camera I knew I'd been right. Its feel in my hand was as it should have been. I was sure that when I got the chance to look, I'd find no killer laser, no beautifully miniaturized power pack.

I followed the private.

"Kuba," the corporal's voice came after us, "when he is ready, drive Mr. Pike wherever he wishes to go."

He was turning me loose, and with few questions. Why?

I turned in the doorway. "Thank you," I started to say, then, remembering the local reaction to thanks, stopped myself in the middle of the phrase.

The corporal looked up. "Yes?"

"I . . . this Piot Kval, am I supposed to know him?" I said.

"It is of no consequence," the corporal said. "If the name is not known to you, it is not known to you."

His voice was an unmistakable dismissal and I was glad to take the hint, even though I felt uneasy. I thought of it, but I did not search my clothes for hidden carrier-beam transmitters when Kuba brought them to me, clean and dry.

"My wrist-chrono," I said. "I had a wrist-chrono."

Kuba tapped my sleeve pocket and, when I groped in it, my fingers touched my timepiece.

"Thank you," I said without thinking.

"Thanks are not necessary," Kuba said, but I was already nodding that I knew.

41

He left me and I was glad to be alone to struggle with my clothes and my great weariness.

Piot Kval, I thought to myself as I waited for a rise in the strength of my hands. My clothes were clean, and they were dry. But they were also stiffened and rough and they smelled highly of the ever-present *Poldrogi* disinfectant.

Piot Kval. And the corporal with the cold eyes seemed to feel that I ought to know him.

Piot Kval . . . and my fingerprints on a record.

No, not fingerprints, finger*print*.

Fingerprint! And I had an idea.

Finger*print!*

A great wave of queasiness surged up to take me over. I fought it down. Rest. I needed rest.

Rest . . . and sleep . . . and a chance for my body to clear itself of shock . . . stop this dreadful hum in my head. . . .

I dressed, and when I was ready, went looking for Kuba and the promised ride home.

Home. The transhaus and its sleep cubicle . . . and my thumb*print* on the safebox at the foot of my bunk.

I might have been wrong, my hearing at a low point, but I was sure the corporal had said "print" and not "prints." And the transhaus was the only place that I knew that had required a record of just my one thumbprint.

Not as a record in itself, but as a pattern for the safebox lock to record electronically, and to recognize when it was presented to it again by the simple act of my pressing my thumb against its lockplate.

It was at least a starting point, but it would have to wait.

Wait . . . and sleep first . . . and where was Kuba?

Kuba.

I was proud of the way I could walk without weaving . . . and I resented his hand under my arm.

I yanked my arm away from his support. "I'm all right," I said.

"Yes," he said. "There is a step here . . . and another below that and then we are on the level ground."

I did not thank him.

Weave . . . do not weave when you walk . . . tired . . . else they will keep you . . . must not let them keep you.

The hum . . . the hum in my head.

CHAPTER TEN

I stood on the broad, single step that led up to the transhaus entrance and watched the twin green taillights of the police car skim away from me and get smaller and smaller and closer and closer together.

I shook my head and I turned ... and they were waiting for me. Two of them, stepping from the shadow at one side of the slowly revolving door.

I blinked at them. They were familiar yet I'd never seen them before, of that I was sure.

And the hard pressure on my ribs as they came up on either side of me was familiar too ... and that I *had* felt before.

The taller one's weapon, pointed at me, even through a pocket, should have made me afraid.

But it didn't. All I felt was a great weariness and a kind of sad indignation at being put upon for so long, being kept, it would seem, from the rest I'd earned and wanted so badly.

He was taller than his friend, but still short against my six-feet-four. He was young, he was tough, and he was expecting no trouble from me.

I was vastly weary and I was filling up with indignation. In what felt like a kind of syrupy slow motion I turned into him and away from his buddy on my other side. In the turning, my size thirteen foot came down on his and pinned it to the ground so that he could not step away from me.

Had the light been better, I'm sure I would have been very interested in watching my two hands grip the barrel of his weapon through the cloth of his pocket, and twist.

Twist outward, in a way that his fingers could not bend. Or maybe they could be made to at that. His yelp in my ears was only a kind of obbligato to the snap I heard, muted of course, that seemed to go with the loosening of his grip.

But the light was good enough for me to see my left hand slide along his right arm and into his pocket and emerge, slightly sticky and red-bedaubed, with a stubby handgun.

My hand and the gun did not stop moving. Idly, I watched

their slow progress upward, upward until the gun rested under the young man's chin.

It rested, or at least it looked to me like it did, but I could have been wrong because his head raised up and the gun slid on past his lip and nose.

Red again. On the chin, on the lip, on the nose. But color is hard to tell in dim light. It could be brown ... or even green. No, I had a feeling for color. My first impression had been that it was red. I'd stay with that. Red.

Tired. He seemed suddenly to be as tired as I was. His eyes closed very slowly, the dark pupils rolling upward and back, so that only the whites were left for the heavy lids to slip down over.

He floated. Like a huge toy settling to the bottom of a child's play pool he settled to the transhaus step.

His weapon was still in my hand. I stared at it. Red. It was red all right, and I felt a glow of pleasure warming me. It was nice to know that you could trust your first impression to be right ... especially about a thing that mattered in your work. Color. ... Color *is* important to a photographer in his work.

I stared at the gun, kept staring, trying to think what I could possibly want with it. My eyes followed along its barrel, outward, upward ... and I was looking at the young man's friend.

He had his right hand inside his tunic front and he seemed to be frozen in that position.

I made a little circle with his friend's gun point, chiefly to reassure him that my first flush of indignation at being kept from a well-deserved rest was over. I was sorry, of course, but he could see my point, couldn't he?

He said nothing and then I realized that neither had I for that matter. I'd been doing all my talking in my head.

But his hand was coming out very slowly from the front of his tunic.

His tunic. Now I knew why he and his friend had looked familiar at first sight. It was blue and yellow.

A blue-and-yellow business tunic. Plagiar's colors. Of course, he and his friend were two of Anton Plagiar's bully boys ... and I'd treated them very shabbily.

His hand was free of his blue-and-yellow tunic and very gingerly holding the mate to the gun in my own hand. He laid it gently on the ground then, slowly, and for some reason never taking his eyes from the gun in my hand, he started to ease away from me.

44

With my empty hand I waved him to come back and then pointed to his friend resting so comfortably, it looked to me, on the broad step.

His eyes never leaving me, he moved in, slipped his hands under his friend's armpits and, puffing more than was necessary, it seemed to me, dragged him off, his heels trailing, and into a small black-and-white skimmer I now saw parked a short distance off.

Black-and-white. It's not too far away, but the light there is even poorer than it is here. It could be a dark ... no, stay with your first impression. You were right about the red. You're right this time too. Black-and-white it is.

Green. The taillights are green, but that's not fair because they light up from inside. Besides, they're out of sight now anyway.

Anton Plagiar's bully boys. What did they want?

I became aware of a weight in my hand and brought my eyes to a focus on it.

A handgun. What did I want with a laser-beam handgun?

It felt sticky, and the red on it was all up and down the sleeve of my jumpsuit. And after the police had just gone to all that trouble to clean it for me too.

I shrugged and looked around for a place to throw the gun. None seemed about to present itself, so I loosened my grip on the gun butt and let it fall right where I stood.

It landed with a clatter and a sound of solid metal striking. Interesting, I thought. You'd expect to hear the solid sound first and then the clatter.

Or maybe that was the way it had been. The thud and then the clatter. Or was it the clatter and *then* the thud?

It was easy enough to find out, just drop the gun again and listen closely this time.

But to do that I'd have to stoop down to pick it up.

Stoop down.

I considered that and the gun at my feet for a long, long time. Then I shrugged. What was the difference if I couldn't keep a sequence of sounds straight. I was great on colors wasn't I?

I turned and made my way into the transhaus through its slowly revolving doors. My head. Would the blasted humming in it never ease up?

CHAPTER ELEVEN

He was following me, I was sure of it now, and it made me nervous.

I had a right to be nervous.

The spattering of blood, dry and brown now, on my sleeve. I must have been out of my head to take on two of Plagiar's bully boys. Two, with guns, and me, my bare hands and no brains.

I shook my head. It felt better now and, when I flexed my fingers, the phasing of their strength was more of an annoyance than an actual hazard.

But the man dogging me was making me nervous. I could have turned and walked up to him and asked him point blank what he had in his mind, but how could I know what he had in those hands deep in his baggy pockets; and the way I was looking at it right now, I'd just about used up all the luck any mortal was reasonably entitled to in my scuffle last night with Plagiar's men.

He was tall, and fairly broad, and his hair was as white as Plagiar's, but he wore it cut short and standing straight up. And he had glasses. Thick, dark-rimmed, Earthside glasses.

Somehow, I had the feeling that he'd come out of the transhaus only shortly before I did.

I eased my record camera out of my sleeve pocket, cocked and aimed it over my shoulder, backward and hidden in my palm.

I made the exposure, and slipped the camera back into my sleeve pocket, noting the picture's number in the tiny tab window so that I could play it back for the transhaus clerk to look at if I got the chance.

The transhaus clerk. He was an antiseptic-looking youth I didn't remember having seen before.

"Where's the manager?" I'd asked him when I came up from my sleep cubicle and stopped in for my receipted sleep-bill, and to ask about a place to eat.

"He is my uncle," the boy said. "We have not seen him these twenty-four hours and we are greatly concerned."

46

"Oh?" I said, and I thanked him for the directions to a nearby gasthaus that served food at all hours.

"No thanks are necessary," he told me, and it began to dawn on me that this was the *Poldrogi* way of expressing a simple "you're welcome."

Almost as an afterthought, I turned back from the revolving door. "What's your uncle's name?" I asked the boy.

"Kval," he said. "Piot Kval."

Piot Kval. The manager of the transhaus where I slept, and I had told the police I didn't know the man.

The corporal was entitled to his skeptical look, it would appear. And I had no doubt at all that if Kval stayed missing very much longer, the corporal would let his attitude of disbelief change to something more unpleasant for me than just an attitude.

Twenty-four hours. *Poldrogi's* very rapid day-and-night sequence made it confusing for an off-worlder to keep track of time, but twenty-four hours ago . . . ?

I checked off the hours in my head. Twenty-four would take it back to just about the time that Brigit had been in Kval's office and waiting for me.

But he was not there when I saw her, so that I might very well have been the last person to talk to him when he'd come to awaken me and tell me of Brigit.

And the questioning of me by the police suddenly took on a nasty point.

Kval was out of his office, but Brigit expected him back, else why did she leave the two double-eagles on his desk for him?

Or maybe she had good reason to know that he wouldn't be back and the double-eagles were a subterfuge . . . to fool me.

Forty dollars worth of subterfuge? I shook my head. I fooled cheaper than that.

But she had seen him, he'd said she had . . . and if he turned up completely vanished or dead, I had a sinking feeling I knew who would be near the top of the police list of prime suspects.

And I also knew that escape from the planet was out of the question. I didn't have the money for standard passage . . . and stowing away would let me stay aboard ship only until the first search-robot nosed past my would-be hiding place.

Brigit. I had to find out for the sake of my own neck what that gambit at the Wayfarer's Home was all about.

Some killer had tried to make of me a patsy . . . and someone had nearly nailed me with a masher beam. A camera that should have been smashed was as perfect as when it was new.

And the bully boys. If the blood on my sleeve was any indication, I'd somehow managed to cut up one of them elsewhere than in just his pride . . . and I had no hope that either of them was of the forgive-and-forget school of thought.

And I was hungry. Lord, was I hungry. Except for the hot drink at the police barracks that my phasing stomach refused to hold, I'd had no food since before meeting Brigit.

Brigit . . . and Plagiar . . . but first of all, food.

I let the slowly revolving door of the transhaus carry me through and it was then that I noticed the tall man with the straight-up hair and the heavy glasses begin to take off after me.

CHAPTER TWELVE

I flicked on the gasthaus table radio and listened to the newscast while I shoveled food into my mouth. When they came around to the weather prediction for the second time and still hadn't mentioned the brouhaha at the Wayfarer's Home, or that one of their citizens was missing, I turned it off.

But I did not stop eating and it was only when I was about two-thirds of the way through the second portion that the table-boy had brought me that I looked up from my work to eye the tall man at the far end of the room who was making a poor job of not looking at me through his heavy-rimmed glasses.

He'd taken more than a decent interval to come into the gasthaus after me and he sat alone at his round table now, worrying the one large cup of local tea he'd picked up, and getting very hard stares from his table-boy.

The food in my stomach was having its effect, and he didn't look quite so menacing. In fact, now that I was pointedly staring at him as I ate, I saw that he was beginning to fidgit.

Or, if not actually fidgit, then twitch in his seat like a man with something on his mind that he would rather not have there. A fish out of water, a man over his depth.

He hunched around in his seat until his back was toward me, and I saw his head bobbing slightly up and down as though he were talking to somebody. Only there was nobody in the chair opposite him at the table.

Then abruptly he shoved back both his chair and his cup and got up, all at the same time and almost in the same motion, and he was coming directly toward me with a deep scowl on his face.

He stopped so close that he had his small pot of a stomach almost in my face. I don't like a pepper-and-salt pattern, and I like it even less up against my snout. His baggy jumpsuit had a musty smell to it, like something locked up and long forgotten.

"Sklar," he said in a voice that was almost belligerent. "I'm Dr. Rolf Sklar. May I sit down?"

He said the name as though it ought to mean something to me. It didn't. And I didn't like his stomach in my face.

Or maybe it was just that it was my belly that was full. "You can drop dead if you like, friend," I said and dropped my eyes back to my plate.

I'd dropped my eyes, but I'd seen the flicker of a pained look in his face, and I realized that his belligerence could very well be directed, not at me, but at himself. Here was indeed a fish out of its element.

I'm sorry, Doctor, I said in my head. But aloud I said nothing. I just let him stand there while I went on eating.

He took a long time deciding, but when he did I heard him let out his breath in a gasping wheeze.

On the rim of my vision I saw him reach into the inside pocket of his baggy jumpsuit and come up with something that he laid on the table in front of me.

My eyes couldn't help flicking up to it, but I had them back on my plate in an instant.

He sighed and opened the folded-over bit of thick paper and flattened it out with long, spadelike fingers.

Circles. I didn't read the first digit, but the zeros that came after it impressed me. A sight-draft for five figures. Ten thousand Earth credits and maybe more if I was willing to appear interested enough to actually look at the first digit closely enough to make it out.

I didn't look.

He sighed again, this time with a quavering sound. "It's all I have," he said. "All I could get together. Tell me where the boy is."

I felt myself sweating, and it wasn't all the fault of *Poldrogi's* heat or the suddenly stuffy air of the gasthaus.

This was a man who thought I knew something ... and something valuable enough to lay out five figures worth of credits for.

"You have got the wrong table," I said. "I don't know what you're talking about."

He pulled back the chair opposite and slammed himself down into it. "Look," he said, right into my face, "I'm not a devious man. This is all the cash I have and it's all there is, and I might just be giving you a way out. Think about that."

Cheese. That local green cheese with the heavy streaks of

50

white-and-blue mold running through it. He'd had cheese for breakfast.

"I still don't know what you're talking about," I said.

"I said I'm not a devious man and I'm not, but I was out at the Wayfarer's Home yesterday and I saw what happened."

He let his voice trail off and sat looking at me as though what he'd just said was supposed to have a special meaning for me.

It did, but not what he thought it should have, I'd have been willing to bet.

It was starting to occur to me that maybe that sniper's shot at me wasn't a lucky near-miss at all. That I'd been set up as a patsy, but not for an assassination attempt. This could be the reverse play.

I'd been thinking that someone had wanted to kill Plagiar and then nail me before I could be arrested and talked to.

It could very well be that the sniper didn't want Plagiar dead and had never intended to hit me. That the only intent had been to make me look important enough to kill.

Important enough to kill and so important enough to contact and offer money to for information about a boy.

Important enough to be a red herring across somebody else's trail.

And it had worked, else why was this agitated man sitting opposite me, leaning so close and peering at me through his thick glasses?

But where did a missing transhaus manager fit in? And the green dye that had almost gotten me lynched by a mob? And Plagiar's bully boys . . . do not forget Plagiar's bully boys.

I shook my head and Sklar misunderstood the motion. He snatched up his sight-draft and jammed it into his inside pocket. "All right," he said. "Have it your way. I said that I'm not a devious man and I'm not. If you live long enough to change your mind I'm staying at the Matruza."

He slammed back his chair and was stalking out of the gasthaus before that crack about living long enough to change your mind made its way past my ears and into my head.

I was still shaking my head when I looked up from staring into my plate and saw that I was about to have another visitor.

Bearing down on me, mouth all pulled down and dark eyes intense looking, was Brigit.

51

Brigit Plagiar ... and behind her were two bully boys and one of them had pale skin patched on his chin, his lip, and his nose; his right hand stiff with splints and bandages.

CHAPTER THIRTEEN

Anger? Fear? Anxiety? I tried to read the look on Brigit's face as she drew closer to me, the bully boys making a kind of counterpoint backstop to divide my scrutiny.

And then, suddenly, her face was pleasant, but uninterested; and the two bully boys were just a couple of stocky young men in blue-and-yellow tunics pulling back chairs and looking around for a table-boy.

And then I heard it too, the double-tone beeping of police vehicles, and coming to a stop out front.

I caught at Brigit's wrist as she came close and started to move on past me. She did not resist, did not try to pull away. She stood there, face pleasant, still looking straight ahead until I released my grip. Then she went on to a table close by the kitchen door as if she'd never broken her stride since first she'd stepped into the gasthaus.

The police corporal. I recognized him even with his bald head hidden under a uniform cap. He stopped by my table but did not sit down. He seemed no friendlier than the last time I'd seen him, but then he seemed no more hostile either.

"Mr. Pike," he said. "I would like to speak with you."

"Sit down," I said, pushing the leftovers on my plate around with some pretense of not being finished with my breakfast.

"Elsewhere," he said.

"Am I under arrest?" I asked.

There was only the briefest of pauses before the corporal said, "May I see your identification, please."

My identification card . . . my card case. My card case . . . my CE license.

I pushed back my chair and stood up. "I read you," I said. "Loud and clear."

The corporal did not flicker an eyelid. "This way, please," he said, and I followed him outside the gasthaus.

Three police skimmers? Just to pick up one ex-SpaceNav Photo Mate? It didn't seem possible.

It wasn't.

"One moment, please," the corporal said, and walked to the last skimmer in the line to lean inside it for a moment.

When he came back he was draping a small gray box on a lanyard around his neck. He slid the tiny black control button on its side downward to the lock position and the square window that was a kind of lid to the box glowed amber.

A signal damper.

It gave off no audible sound and would not interfere with airborne vibrations, but any electronic pickup within the small sphere of its unheard signal would deliver back at its home end nothing more than a crackling, undecipherable hiss.

I looked around. Who did he think would be listening in on us out here?

But the corporal was speaking to me. "Come," he said, "it is not far."

It wasn't. Only the retracing of the brief distance I'd come from the transhaus.

The clerk, when I'd spoken to him earlier, had looked young to be substituting for his uncle. Now, sitting against the wall with a police private in the chair behind the desk, he looked barely into his teens. And when he led us down the ramp to the first level below the field surface, his head, seen from behind, seemed to waggle and dip as though it were too large and too heavy for its shaved neck to carry. He was blond, as I suppose his bald uncle might once have been.

His uncle, the fat manager. He came to the end of the corridor and the boy slid open a panel marked with a scrubbed and faded "B." He stepped back, his face turned away.

His uncle, the fat manager. Something pressed into a corner, the fat shoulders held upright by the angle of the walls, arms and legs sprawling.

A stain, small, almost lost in the larger, faded ones on the T shirt that had the color of dry and faded blood.

A stain, small and under the heart. A laser wound that bled little since its killer beam, searing as it pierced, locked in all but an ooze.

"How long?" I asked, but I already knew the answer.

"He's been dead some thirty-six hours, give or take a few," the corporal said. "We'll pin it down later. The boy found him when he came down for a refill cylinder for their disinfecting system."

And now I noticed that the room was small and obviously used for the storage of dull, squat, gas-cylinder shapes.

The corporal was eyeing the blood spatters on the sleeve of my jumpsuit. "Do you still deny knowing him?" he asked.

I tugged at my sleeve. "This isn't his blood," I protested. "I didn't have it when he was killed. You know that. You cleaned this suit yourself."

"I asked if you still deny knowing him?"

"No, I don't deny it. I wouldn't have denied it yesterday if you'd told me who he was. I only found out his name an hour ago."

The corporal shrugged. "Yesterday I was asking about a man who'd been gone only a matter of hours. A favor for an employer who had a job he should have been filling. An employer who would have thought it no favor if by seeming to press with my questions I should give rise to rumors. A missing manager, even if no funds are gone with him . . . a statement many would have their own ideas about . . . cannot help but reflect on the rest of a man's establishment."

"This," I said, pointing at the dead man, "this is going to help his business?"

"Ah," said the corporal. "This we must assume his employer did not know about."

The boy who had guided us to the storeroom stood, his back to us, ramrod straight. The corporal touched his shoulder. "All right, Fraan," he said. "You can go back to work now."

The boy left without so much as looking back.

"They lived alone," the corporal said, his voice unexpectedly sympathetic. "Perhaps now that his uncle is gone he will go back to his home world." He shook his head and in the same sympathetic tone of voice said to me, "What did the doctor want for his twenty thousand credits?"

"He said . . . ," and then I caught myself. "I didn't know what he was talking about," I said. I might not tell the corporal all I could remember of what Dr. Rolf Sklar had said to me, but he was no man I wanted to start lying to either.

Twenty thousand. Twenty thousand credits. I had purposely kept my eyes averted from Sklar's sight-draft, but the quick glimpse I'd had of it . . . I played the row of five figures back in my head . . . no, that first figure hadn't looked like a two.

Aloud I said, "How did you know he offered me anything at all?"

The corporal did not answer me. "I make no threats, Mr. Pike," he said. "I merely point out that you were here when Piot was killed . . . or at least the time sheet upstairs would indicate that he made no entry to check you out when you left . . ."

Time sheet. Transhaus sleep cubicles. You paid for them in advance . . . and by the hour . . . as you used them. If you had an hour between starships and wanted to spend it resting up after the bout of warp-sickness you'd just been through, you checked into a transhaus.

Nothing could be handier to a spaceport than its transhaus accommodations. Accommodations whose skeleton went in even before the sub-structure of the field itself was laid down. You had to house your workers somewhere and it was easier and less demanding of expensive building materials to dig a hole and maintain it than to erect comparably-sized above-ground facilities.

And after your construction crews debarked for other planets and other jobs, they left behind ready-made housing that, while not fancy, couldn't have been any handier.

And, because the time needs varied so greatly, there never were, and never had been any arbitrary day-minimums, or even noon-to-midnight charges. If you stayed an hour, you paid for an hour. If you were a photographer who was watching his credits, you checked in to sleep . . . and you checked out . . . and when you did, you checked out with the manager to make sure that you hadn't overstayed your de-clared-and-paid-for time.

Piot Kval hadn't checked me out; might even have been dead when I followed Brigit out of his office.

Brigit . . . and forty dollars left for a dead man.

I became aware of the silence and realized that the corporal was waiting for me to answer the question he'd just put to me.

Fingerprints . . . it was something about fingerprints . . . did I deny that the print on the safebox lockplate was mine? Was it, perhaps, a clever forgery?

I shook my head. No, I did not deny that. Early in their use, it had been discovered that the lockplate, which scruti-nized electronically the pattern of ridges and whorls on the thumb presented to it when its lid was closed, could be opened by simply presenting the same pattern in the shape of

56

a print lifted from a water glass ... or even a one-to-one photograph.

Redesigning of the device was immediate, and now the record included a reading of the electrical potential of the skin that formed the ridges so that the thumb presented had at least to be alive. Still, boxes were being opened, and the tug-of-war between designer and thief was a continuing one.

"Thirty-six hours ago I was here," I said to the corporal. "I was here and I spoke to the manager. He called me to an assignment and the last I saw of him he was walking away from me and back to his office for all I know."

"Ah, yes, the assignment. The affair at the Wayfarer's Home."

"Yes," I said, and I wondered if I ought to tell him to verify my story with Brigit, that she too had been there. But if she'd had anything to do with Kval's death, she'd hardly own up to it, and her denial would just make any statement of mine that much less plausible, and me that much more suspect.

Suspect. So far the corporal hadn't made any specific accusation, just seemed bent on making me out a liar.

"And the twenty thousand credits ... what was that for?"

It was the second time he'd asked that question. "I've already told you," I said. "I have no idea what Sklar was talking about ... I didn't even know his name until he told me what it was ... and I still don't know who he is."

The corporal held up a pudgy hand. "I do not mean to try your patience, Mr. Pike, but let us consider.

"You are a photographer, not well known and of ... ," he looked about him at the scrubbed and faded transhaus walls, ". . . of less than affluent means. Yet you are singled out to photograph a man of no little prominence ... a distinguished visitor.

"You are bedaubed by a dye we use only for riots ... yet none of my men has done this to you. They, in fact, must rescue you from a mob pursuing you for reasons none can describe now, except in the vaguest of terms. They thought you a menace to their children ... and no one can remember who first raised the cry against you.

"You have told me that you were fired upon by a sniper and there is evidence that some weapon was indeed used. But it is not evidence of a masher beam, Mr. Pike. It is evidence of a cutting laser ... and from its angle it came from no distant point, but rather from the platform itself. The platform, Mr. Pike, that you were on."

I started to protest, but the corporal showed me his palm again.

"Furthermore, a citizen on his way to work finds two pistols and spatters of blood on the step of your transhaus, and its manager is found dead in a storeroom, killed, it would appear, at a time that you have just admitted to being on his premises."

He pointed at my sleeve. "You have blood on a sleeve that we both know was clean less than twelve hours ago.

"A man is seen waiting outside a bank for it to open so that he can transfer all of his funds into a draft account and shortly afterward this same man is heard offering it all to you for information you tell him, and now me, that you do not have."

Heard? Sklar was heard talking to me? He hadn't particularly kept his voice down, but there simply hadn't been time for anyone to have passed the information on to the corporal ... or to anyone else for that matter. Sklar had left, and the police had come on the scene almost at once ... and no one had made a hurried exit that I'd seen.

The corporal was still pegging his points at me. "The doctor did not seem to believe that your ignorance was genuine ... gave you his address at the Matruza ... should you change your mind."

I goggled at the corporal. He had the exact words.

He went on coldly, but almost ruefully. "For a man who claims innocence and ignorance, you have been subjected to a singular series of happenings."

And then his voice went unmistakably flat. "All right, Pike, do you want to tell me what is really going on? The falling out of thieves? Did your partner get a little greedy, Pike? Or did he get scared when he found out how big a man your intended victim is ... and it was silence him or drop the whole enterprise?

"But that isn't the most unfortunate part is it, Pike? The most unfortunate part is now. Now that the whole affair has curdled, you are still as lacking of funds as you ever were .. and you cannot accept any that might fall your way for fear of breaking the mask of innocence ... of ignorance, you have selected to wear. Tell me, Pike, what does Sklar want for his twenty thousand?"

"I don't know!" I shouted, and I didn't know if I was angry or dismayed at the unbelievability of my predicament.

58

"I don't know. I don't know what he was talking about. I don't know who killed Kval. I don't know what is going on. I don't know."

The corporal was suddenly laughing, a nasty sound. "Have it your way," he said. "There are others in this with you and I frankly expect you to deny all . . . but I will not take you with me. I want only for the moment to give to the others a sense of some urgency when they think of you."

I could feel the scar on the top of my head begin to prickle. "What . . . what are you driving at?" I said to the corporal.

"Always the pretense of ignorance, is it not so, Mr. Pike? Very well, I will enlighten you. You do not, then, know of the transmitter in your wrist-chrono?"

I stared at the tiny timepiece on my wrist. "A transmitter? In my wrist-chrono?"

"In the stem, to be exact. Our laboratory discovered it when they went over your clothes while you were our guest."

I looked up at him. "But who . . . ?"

He chuckled, another unpleasant sound. "It is an interesting question for you to ponder on. Who indeed? It is a tiny unit and not large enough for a really complex scrambler, so that we were able to break its pattern with very little trouble. I heard you speaking to the doctor, Mr. Pike, but who else also did?"

He fingered the gray shape of the signal damper glowing on the lanyard around his neck. "What I say to you now, have said to you since we were together, has not been heard by anyone, of course, and it has perhaps set them to wondering. It is my hope that it is so."

He smiled at me, showing me hand-carved teeth like those of the dead Kval. "You see, Mr. Pike, I am setting you up as a . . ." he groped for the word, " . . . decoy? No, that is not the word . . . one of those things that is shot at . . . a duck . . . a sitting duck. Yes, Mr. Pike. I am setting you out as a sitting duck to be shot at in the hope that the hunter will thus betray himself."

Decoy . . . duck . . . he was splitting hairs. I stared, fascinated, at the timepiece on my wrist.

"It does present something of a problem, doesn't it, Mr. Pike. Should you leave your transmitter where it is and have your every word, your very breathing listened to by whom? Where? Or should you tear it out and cut your betraying link? But if you do that, Mr. Pike, then you will also break your link to me ... your listener will not be able to hear you, but then neither will I, should he drive you into a corner from which there is no escape."

He seemed now to be genuinely enjoying himself. "You have an interesting decision to make, Mr. Pike. An interesting decision."

He put a thumb on the tiny black control button of his signal damper. "And now, Mr. Pike, the best of luck," and he slid the button up and into the "off" position.

The amber light behind its small window went out and I knew that my every movement, my every mutter would carry and be heard where? By whom?

The corporal touched a finger to the peak of his uniform cap and walked away from me toward the end of the corridor. Just before he went out of sight he turned, showed me his teeth again.

"Quack, quack," he said and his cold chuckle as he went up the ramp was loud enough to carry back to me.

To me, standing, staring at the stem of my wrist-chrono, rubbing unabashedly at the scar on my head.

Who? Where? And just when had they had the chance to plant it to begin with? How long had I been carrying it? Hours ago? Or planets ago?

How long has someone had his finger on me?

CHAPTER FOURTEEN

Anton Plagiar raised an eyebrow at me. "My wife? When did you ever meet my wife?" His tone was ordinary enough, but again I sensed the latent power of the man.

I glanced uncertainly around the sitting room of his hostel suite, at the two bully boys standing easy at the anteroom door, the new skin patches on the face of the taller one very prominent in my eyes at the moment; the fingers of his hand, stiff in their splints and bandages, inescapable.

"I . . . she hired me. She hired me to take pictures of you during your magic act."

He laughed, but it was a short laugh and not one that sounded amused at all. "I haven't seen my wife for months. And the last thing she'd want is a photograph of me and my childish little performance."

"But," I said, and I wondered what kind of a trap I had talked myself into walking into. My wrist-chrono that was a direct line to the listener, but also to the corporal if I got into a bind, was carefully locked in the safebox at the foot of my transhaus bunk.

I'd had a feeling of satisfaction that bordered on the smug when that gambit had finally dawned on me. The corporal had thought to leave me with the hard choice of leaving the transmitter where it was and risk a betrayal through the sounds that I made myself or what might be said to me, or tear it out and thus warn the listener that I knew of him and perhaps bring him down on me from a quarter I could not begin to suspect, his identity unknown to me.

What was simpler, though, than to leave the transmitter untouched but to deceive the one who listened?

Brigit. Brigit had seemed to me to be the one with answers I needed desperately to know, so I waited until it was believably late enough, faked the sounds of turning in and then, leaving my timepiece behind, had come as unobtrusively as I could to the hostel at which I'd expected to find her.

I hadn't hoped that I could avoid Plagiar and speak to

Brigit alone, but neither had I expected to face him on as confusing a basis as this one.

He laughed, but now he did sound amused, and I thought I heard a snicker from the bully boys by the door. He motioned with his hand, pointing at an inner door, and one of the bully boys vanished through it.

He was back in a moment and the woman with him was Brigit.

"Brigit," Plagiar said, "did you hire this man to take pictures of me?"

Brigit settled herself in a corner of one of the room's several sofas. "Yes and no," she said. "I thought it might be well to have him where we could see him when I heard that Sklar had been recognized. I knew that he couldn't refuse if I told him I was your wife."

Refuse? She hadn't given me a chance to. We were in her skimmer and on our way before she told me who she was.

Plagiar smiled, but at the same time he shook his head. "Some day, Brigit, your little habit of not bothering me with details is going to make me very unhappy with you."

He turned his attention to me. "Sklar offered you twenty thousand. I'll double his figure. Where is the boy?"

I shook my head. I wasn't answering him, I was just trying to clear it. The corporal, and now both Brigit and Plagiar, all either taking for granted, or trying to force, a relationship between me and a man I had never seen, never even heard of until scant hours ago.

Twenty thousand. The same figure that the corporal had used, yet I was sure that it was a wrong one. Could Plagiar have it from the same source as the corporal? Was he the listener?

If he was, oughtn't he to have looked a little surprised to see a man he thought to be in his bunk and asleep? He hadn't, but then would a man get to be as powerful as he if he had a face that showed anything but what he wanted it to show?

I was shaking my head and Plagiar made a small gesture of impatience. "All right. Fifty thousand, but I warn you, I intend to have the boy."

Protesting that I didn't know what they were talking about had gotten me exactly nowhere with anyone, but I would give it one more go.

"I don't know what you're talking about," I said to Plagiar, and my luck with the flat statement was no better than before.

He nodded. "A very sensible attitude to take, but you'll understand if I find it hard to believe that it was sheer coincidence that you should stay at Kval's establishment ... or that it was just a case of mistaken identity that led someone to try for you with a masher beam. I might add that for a moment my men mistook your firing back with your camera gun as an attempt on me, until they saw that when it jammed you fought to keep it pointed downward."

He smiled and looked at his bully boys. "I'm sorry about the dye," he said. "But a police weapon that does not kill often avoids a serious probing, yet it can be remarkably effective."

All right. So the bully boys shot at me by mistake. But who raised the cry afterward that sent the mob after me? Or was that a mistake too? Hardly. I had the feeling of pressures within pressures, of attacks within attacks. And who had cleaned up my camera for the police?

But Plagiar was answering that. "A weapon in your camera," he was saying, "how venerable a device. But I do not mean to criticize. I took the liberty of having it removed for fear that if the police found it they might jump to a completely unwarranted conclusion that could only cause misunderstanding and embarrassment all around."

If you took it out, you know it wasn't a simple jamming ...

"Thank you," I said, and there was complete silence while we all stared at each other.

I broke it with the first thing that came into my mind.

"Kval is dead," I said.

"Yes," Plagiar nodded. "Frankly, I did not recognize him, he'd grown so fat . . . and what a name to assume, Kval, *Smith*. It is enough to arouse suspicion on any planet. But that he should be killed did surprise me . . . until I learned of you."

We were back to me again . . . and now, in their minds, I was tied to a man who'd had reason to hide his once-thin body under layers of fat . . . and his real name behind the one of *Smith*, Kval.

And *he* was dead.

I'd come looking for Brigit and for some answers. I'd also come, because, remembering the bully boys and the transhaus step, I'd half reasoned it might go easier to confront Plagiar before he issued a second invitation.

So now I knew who'd cleaned up my camera but not who planted the laser.

I knew that if Plagiar hadn't heard of me until *after* Kval was dead then *he* hadn't planted the transmitter ... and he wasn't the listener.

I didn't know who had ... and I didn't know when.

Least of all did I know why.

The boy. Worth fifty thousand now. Fifty thousand!

Who was he? And why did everyone seem to be so positive that I knew where he was?

Plagiar was looking at me ... Brigit was looking at me.

I turned. The two bully boys by the door were looking at me.

And Kval, who might have known, was dead.

I made a move toward the door, but neither of the bully boys looked as though he had any mind to step aside for me.

I turned back to Plagiar. I tried not to think that my line to the corporal was out ... out when I'd left the transmitter off my wrist ... that I'd taken some small pains to take leave of the transhaus without being seen. Who knew I was in Plagiar's suite? Had ever been, if *I* turned up missing.

I cleared my throat. I had only one bargaining point. And that one had a validity only as long as Plagiar believed what I knew wasn't so. That I knew the whereabouts, if not the identity, of some as yet unnamed "boy."

And it was dawning on me that, valid or no, it was the only bargaining point I did have.

"I'll think about it," I said to Plagiar, and knew that by those words I'd affirmed as true something I knew wasn't so. "I'll have to think about it. Fifty thousand is a lot of money."

Plagiar did not move and neither did his bully boys, and the sweltering air of *Poldrogi* indoors was suddenly very chill to me.

He spoke, and it seemed to be completely off the subject.

"Pike," he said, "how did you find me?"

"You're a big man," I said. "All I had to do was ask."

"Remember that when you think, Pike. Remember that fifty thousand is a lot of money ... and that I'm a big man."

I nodded. I did not trust myself to speak.

The bully boys stepped aside and I was almost at the doorway when Plagiar called my name.

The bully boys snapped back together to block my path at once.

"It has just struck me," Plagiar said, "that I might be

64

misinterpreting your interest in Kval ... or his in you. This will take but a moment, and it will ease my mind about you. You will indulge me?"

He'd put it as a question, but I knew an order when I heard one.

I didn't say anything, I didn't nod, I just stood there.

At Plagiar's nod, Brigit and a bully boy left the room and when they came back he was pushing what looked like an oversize magician's taboret on wheels.

From the way it moved, it looked heavy. Too extravagant of weight to be anything but a major illusion.

Brigit pushed it close to me, and I searched her face for some inkling of what Plagiar had in mind, but she did not lift her eyes from the rolling tabletop in front of her.

The unit was upright and about the size of a large trunk standing on end. Its broad top was unmarred except for a slit some two inches long, and a yellow-metal disk about the size of a double-eagle coin, set about an inch below the surface.

"Touch it," Plagiar said.

I looked at him.

"Touch it," he said, pointing to the disk.

I touched it.

There was a rubbing sensation, as though an invisible edge in the disk had scraped across the flesh of my finger pressed against it.

A pause. Long enough for me to feel the blood pound twice in my ears, and then a tiny ding and a card shot up out of the slit to quiver on the end of a slender rod that held it a foot or so above the tabletop.

It was a trey. The trey of diamonds.

All this equipment to produce a single card?

But Plagiar hadn't looked at it. "Thank you," he said. "I knew it was impossible, yet there are always rumors, you know. It was easy enough to check. Thank you again."

He seemed relaxed now, cordial even.

I wasn't.

For some reason, the touching of the taboret and the wait had pulled me up tight enough to twang. And Plagiar's ease of manner didn't soothe me any.

Nor did it help me any to have the taller bully boy, the one with the patches on the parts of his face I'd clipped with his own gun, reach out and push my shoulder with his good hand as I went past him.

He did not send me sprawling, he did not intend to.

He just shoved, and I got his point.

The point and the sound of Plagiar's laughter to follow me through the anteroom and out into the corridor.

Stepping out of the hostel's slowly revolving main door I got another jolt.

Across the night-deserted street and far up it; too far for me to be sure of what I saw even in the glare of the crime-lights, there was a sudden movement. A tall, broad, white-haired figure stepping back or darting out of sight, or maybe the rim of my vision had caught him in a momentary peering forth from a hiding place.

Rolf Sklar? I couldn't be sure.

I searched up and down the street with my eyes. Not a sign of motion. No black-and-white police skimmers, not a single pair of privates in sweaty brown uniforms patrolling their beat.

There was nobody.

Nobody.

I was alone.

CHAPTER FIFTEEN

Rocks.

I had to have a more than sizable assortment of them in my head to be standing here in the dark at the side of the raw country road, waiting for the one person to show up who'd sucked me into this imbroglio to begin with.

Brigit.

The bully boy with the patches on his face had shoved me, hard, when I passed him on my way out of Plagiar's suite, and I was down in the street before I thrust my hands deep into my jumpsuit pockets and felt the tiny stiffness in one of them.

I stopped under the nearest crime-light to read the note. On a scrap of paper that looked like a corner torn from a larger sheet, the message was classic.

I must see you. The road behind the Wayfarer's Home. In an hour.

And it was signed, Brigit.

In an hour, in the dark, and from the hand of the bully boy.

Great.

The word taxi was unknown beyond the limits of the town and the spaceport itself, so I'd ridden as far as I could and walked the rest of the way. It could have taken me an hour, I didn't know, my timepiece was still safely sending its signal from inside the safebox at the transhaus.

Rolf Sklar, whoever he was, seemed sure, at least ten thousand credits' worth, that I knew something that I didn't know.

About the corporal and the police there was no doubt. They *knew* I knew something I didn't know.

And Plagiar. Plagiar hadn't said the words, but he was giving me only the shortest of possible times to make up my mind to tell him what he wanted to know ... and what I didn't know.

In the dark I sighed. All I needed now was for Brigit to hit me with the same line, when she showed up.

If she showed up.

She showed up.

And I got it.

It was dark, but all the same I stared in the direction of her voice.

"You can't mean it," I said. "If anybody should know that I don't even know what they're talking about, it should be you. You picked me out of the air to begin with."

I couldn't make out more than the simple feel of her presence in *Poldrogi's* moonless blackness, but the shrug was plain enough in her off-world-accented voice.

"I did not exactly pick you out of the air, as you say. Your name and your ..." she fumbled for a word, "... your place of staying were given to me."

She had come looking for me, armed with my name and location? But who could know I was on *Poldrogi*, who could even care? There had to be other Pikes ... it was a big galaxy. Some of them named Eli, and some of them even photographers. It had to be a mistake.

I told Brigit so.

She did not contradict me, but from her voice it was plain that she did not believe me any more than did the others.

It was also plain that here was a girl who thought she'd snagged a fish, thrown it back, and then discovered that what she'd taken to be a minnow was really a fat catfish.

A fat catfish.

Me.

She was out to get her hook into me again and her way was one that had worked for centuries ... and would keep on working for centuries to come.

But not tonight.

Not with me.

Not with the things that I had pressing me, no matter how warm the dark night, no matter how great the lure of her scent and the feel of her against me.

I had other things to think about and I didn't need the scar on the top of my head to keep me in mind of them. Lord, but was it itching. And for once I was going to pay it some mind.

I disentangled her arms from around me ... at least I tried to.

"There is money," she was saying against my chest. "More money than you or I can imagine ... can ever dream about. There is power ... there is everything ... everything. ..."

I spoke into her hair. "Why me?" I said. "Why did you come to me?"

I felt her shrug. "It was as I told Anton. It was best that you be where we could see you, except . . ."

"Except what?"

"Except that I did not know when he told me where to find you that Sklar meant for you to die. You must believe me. You must."

And if her arms around me could have matched in their strength, the sincerity of her voice, I would have had a few bruises.

"You must believe I did not know he meant for you to die. I warned you. I tried to warn you when I saw. You must remember that."

I remembered. I remembered her waving on the rim of my vision just as I pressed my camera release and the masher beam whirred past my head.

I remembered her waving, but I'd have to take her word for it that she meant it to be a warning.

"Sklar gave you my name . . . and tried to kill me? So why did he offer me all that money in the gasthaus? Try to shut me up and then offer me all his cash to talk?"

"He did not know then that Kval was dead, and afterward . . . there was only you to go to."

If Sklar did not know that Kval was dead when he took his shot at me then he could not have been the one who killed him. But if Brigit was lying and it hadn't been Sklar sniping, then he could be the killer.

In that case, who'd taken the shot at me . . . and why kill one of the only two men whom you think have information worth . . . what had Brigit said? Money . . . power . . . everything?

Or maybe with two possible sources in mind, whoever'd put the question to Kval hadn't been too careful with him. That left, if the killer thought like Brigit, only me to go to.

Me . . . to keep alive . . . and she was trying her damnedest to weasel the information out of me.

"Tell me," she was repeating over and over . . . in different ways, but it all added up to the same thing. "Tell me where you have hidden the boy and I will go on from there. You will see. Trust me."

I'll bet you would, baby . . . and not hardly.

"Who is the boy?" I asked.

I felt her pull back, perhaps in surprise. "You do not know?"

From what she'd said it would appear that Kval and I were in this together. I took the chance.

"Kval did not tell me," I said. "Why should he?"

I could sense her chewing on that one.

"It is possible," she finally said, and from her voice, she was talking to herself as well as to me. And then, more strongly, and I felt the sudden tensing of her body disappear and she was close to me again. "It is not only possible, but necessary. Kval would have been a fool to tell his accomplice the value of the boy. It is too much ... too much to tempt a man with. No, it was necessary that he lead `you to think it was no more than an ordinary act to work with him."

"You will tell me?" I asked, and I held my breath.

"Yes," she said. "After we have gone to where he is."

I let go my breath. If I was standing up well to her personal brand of temptation, she wasn't about to try me with another kind.

I laughed. "Can you trust me to give you the right boy? Do you know him?"

"Sklar knows him, of course, and Anton has his birth records, childhood pictures, things of that sort ... and the fingerprints from his school records ... and then of course there's the one big test. You saw that."

"Yes," I said. "The one big test."

The one big test? I saw it?

There was a silence between us and I think both of us knew that we'd gone about as far in our exchange as each of us could get the other to go.

She may not have gotten all that she'd arranged the meeting for, but she was sure, I felt, that she'd made her impression on me and that all I needed was a little time to work up a hankering.

And I'd added to my store of things to keep me worried.

"Another time," she said in my ear, and she may have brushed her lips against my cheek in the dark, I couldn't tell from the feel of it. It could just as well have been the touch of a trailing spider tendril or the wind of a night thing passing.

She was gone, along the road from the sound of it. I heard her stumble and give a small gasp, and then the roar of her skimmer stoking up and taking off in the direction of the town.

I shrugged. I might have asked her for a lift to at least the edge of the transportation area if I'd thought of it ... if she hadn't gone so quickly.

70

I settled myself for the long walk ahead of me.

I needn't have.

I walked only a few steps in the blackness and I found out what it was that had made Brigit stumble, made her gasp.

I stumbled over it too.

I fumbled in my sleeve pocket for my record camera. Its flash unit was the only light I had with me, but the split-second bursts would be enough.

I knew *what* I'd stumbled over.

I had to know *who*.

CHAPTER SIXTEEN

It was hot. Hot even for *Poldrogi,* and the police corporal's tunic was drenched with his sweat. On his desk stood his hand-fan, its blades unmoving. "Power," he'd said, conversationally, when his men had brought me in. "Power, it is always a problem. I have used up its power pack and can get no other for I do not know how long. Power and weight, Mr. Pike. Power and weight, they are the problems we of the less favored worlds must cope with."

But he had long since stopped being conversational. "Would it surprise you," he was saying, "if I told you that your fingerprints were on the stone?"

"It sure would surprise me," I said. "I didn't know that a rock could take a print."

"There was blood on this one," he said.

"Blood or no blood, I did not touch the rock ... or the body ... or anything else. I just walked to the Wayfarer's Home and phoned you from there. How many times do you want me to repeat it?"

"And you photographed the body."

"Yes, I photographed the body, but I've already told you why."

"Of course. You wanted to see who it was."

"That's it. I wanted my camera's light to see by."

"And the other picture of the dead man we found when we played back your record. The one of him walking. Was the taking of it also prompted by curiosity?"

The shot of Rolf Sklar following me, the one I'd intended to show the transhaus clerk and never had.

"Yes," I said. "I wanted to know who he was."

"And now you know."

I let that go. I was tired with the heat and the round-and-round sparring with the corporal. And I had an unsettling feeling that a great deal of what I was gleaning from his questions was no slip of his lip. In the back of my head I kept hearing his "quack, quack."

Dr. Rolf Sklar. The "Dr." was honorary. An associate in

72

philosophy at one of the rim-world colleges. A place whose name I'd never heard. That much came from his I.D. card.

The rest . . . what he was doing on *Poldrogi?* . . . and, more to the point, what he was doing on the road where I'd found him? . . . was up in the air.

Sklar, a crumpled heap in the brilliant split-second glare of my flashgun, fallen as though he'd already been in half a crouch when he was struck down.

But no woundless masher beam this, no searing laser. Just a rock, large and heavy, smashed into the back of his skull and then dropped from the killer's hand.

And one other item from the small pile of his personal effects on the desk top in front of the corporal.

A small red box, thin, no larger than a postage stamp.

The corporal had slipped back its lid and pushed it forward for me to look at.

Tiny spindles, almost microscopic in size, each with a pill-shaped swelling at one end, each nested in its fitted pocket of soft foam.

Nine or ten in all, at least two of the pockets empty.

"What are they?" I said, feeling the cushioning softness of the foam with my fingertip.

"You have one in your timepiece," the corporal said. "Transmitters, identical with the one we found in your wrist-chrono."

Without thinking, my eyes flicked to the rest of Sklar's things in front of the corporal. I was looking for a radio, an earpiece, anything that might look as though it could pick up a signal.

"His glasses," I said, remembering their heavy rims, temple pieces. "Did he have a receiver in his glasses?"

The corporal shook his head. "No," he said. "And that leaves you to wonder still who it is that is listening to you." He looked pointedly at my empty wrist. "And he must soon begin to wonder how much sleep you take of a standard day."

Pretty much the same thought had been nagging at me for some time now. I put the box of transmitters back on the corporal's desk. "Are you holding me?" I asked.

He spread his hands. "What for? You found the body of a visitor who died, it would appear, violently. You reported it at once. This was most commendable, particularly since it was necessary for you to brave entering an area that had been less than hospitable to you on your previous visit."

Less than hospitable. The Wayfarer's Home was the only

place anywhere near to me that might have a line into the city when I stumbled over Sklar's body. And doors-with-no-inside-knobs or no, I had a more than public-spirited-citizen urge to keep my nose as clean as I possibly could.

It had occurred to me, not too many microseconds after the flicker of my camera's flashlamps had identified the body at my feet, to wonder if Brigit's gasp, which I'd heard when she stumbled upon the body, had been caused by that simple finding?

Or?

Or had Sklar come with her to what they'd planned to make a trysting place in which she would entice me to give her the information they both seemed to want so badly.

Give it to her and then, my usefulness over, my shield not only vanished, but my existence still knowing what they thought I knew, a menace to them, was it *Sklar* who was to come up behind *me* with a rock?

And if it was, who had pounced upon him . . . and soundlessly?

And what cover story was Brigit rushing to spread to make believable her own slim claim to innocence?

The Wayfarer's Home, a potential trap once I was inside it, had looked suddenly like a haven.

The corporal was talking. " . . . and you have been very patient also with me and my poor, bumbling questions. I thank you."

I answered him in the local idiom. "No thanks are necessary."

He darted me a quick glance and I learned the final reply in the *Poldrogi* ritual of thanks.

"True," he said. "True."

I turned to go, but he had one more thing to say to me. "Kval, if you do not already know, was not the other one's name."

The other one. A man is killed and for the living who must find his killer he is no longer an entity, a person. He is a body, a thing, *the other one.*

"I had heard," I said, remembering Plagiar's amusement that the transhaus manager should have chosen so obvious a name to hide behind. Kval, *Smith.*

"His papers were not authentic, they could not be, but our laboratory was able to detect no difference between them and our own issue. He, or whoever provided him with them, was a forger of an ability I have never before encountered. Baas, his name was, Mahar Baas."

And the corporal waited, his cold eyes under their sweat-beaded brows watching me. I gave no reaction. What reaction was there for me to give? Mahar Baas was as unknown a name to me as had been the one of Piot Kval.

"Where was he from?" I asked.

"Ah," said the corporal. "That is of interest. It would appear that he dropped out of sight some time ago, and with him some equipment the university people seem reluctant to be specific about. At any rate, before he disappeared, Mahar Baas was some sort of laboratory assistant at. . . ."

And he named the planet and the college from which had come the murdered Dr. Rolf Sklar.

CHAPTER SEVENTEEN

Brigit?

Or the boy?

I stood on the broad step of the police barracks, my mind racing.

It is one thing to meet a woman in the dark. It is another to meet her and to know that she, perhaps, means for you to be dead.

But the boy.

Sklar *knew* the boy.

Sklar is dead.

Sklar and Kval. Sklar and Baas ... both from the same planet, the same institution. Baas trying to hide.

Sklar and the transmitters? Nothing.

Baas and the transmitters ... a memory stirring.

A memory of an acrid chemical bite in my nose and throat and of the pounding needed on the panels beside my head to bring me out of a deep sleep.

Before he'd awakened me to tell me of Brigit's presence in his office topside, had Baas cracked a sleep-gas capsule not too close to my face and taken advantage of the few moments so light an exposure would deepen my sleep to reach into the wall pocket behind my head for my timepiece?

But why plant a transmitter on *me*? Had he recognized Brigit, but she not him? Or did they both know fully who the other was, but Baas had an end of his own in mind? A potential double cross?

Or was he acting under instructions from Brigit? ... from Sklar?

I shook my head. Plagiar.

Anton Plagiar. He has the boy's school records, fingerprints, photographs.

He also knows Kval was not Kval but Baas. Knew it before Baas was dead.

Or did he?

He'd said that he didn't know Baas at first under all that

fat. But had he seen him so *before* he was dead ... or *after*?

Before Bass was dead. . . . Then he could not help but know of the boy with him. Fraan, the transhaus-clerk nephew.

But *Sklar* had known and still *he'd* come after me with his offer of money for a boy's whereabouts.

Therefore, Fraan was not the boy Plagiar or Sklar were after.

But Baas had tried to hide his identity behind a false name and under layers of body fat. Could he not have done the same for the boy?

Hormones, perhaps, to hold back a child's growth or to speed it up. Fraan had not looked particularly out of place behind his uncle's desk when I'd first seen him.

Yet, after the discovery of the body, he'd looked strangely immature for the task. Barely into his teens.

A young mind in an artificially matured body?

Plagiar had birth records. Had he ignored Fraan because he did not look to be the right age?

Fingerprints.

Fingerprints and children.

Children ... and institutions ... and a man so obsessed with the finding of a particular child that he'd mounted an elaborate magic show so that he could pursue his search from planet to planet under its suspicion-diverting cloak ... would such a man ignore *any* boy, regardless of age, when all he needed to be sure was to check a fingerprint? Or was it simply a case of checking the ready places first, and the nephew of a transhaus manager would have his turn, but in time.

But if he hadn't known of Baas until *after* he was dead, it was still simple enough to check the prints on anything the boy had touched ... but the death of the uncle had brought the boy to the attention of the police and to spirit him out of sight was to act in the glare of an investigational spotlight ... and big man or no, Plagiar was, after all, not a local ... and he was sensitive. *That* he'd demonstrated by using the magician subterfuge to begin with.

But good enough, he had his finger on the boy, all that was needed now was the patience to wait until the hue and cry died down.

But that brought the usefulness of the knowledge he thought I had to an end ... he no longer had a reason to keep me alive.

If Fraan was the boy they all sought, *nobody* had a reason to keep me alive . . . and any number of reasons to want me dead.

I had to know if the boy and Fraan were the same, to know if my one ace-in-the-hole, blank though the card really was, had any value toward keeping me alive. It is one thing to bluff with a dud card in the hole . . . it is another to try it when you do not even have a hand.

Fingerprints. It would be easy enough to get Fraan's if I did not already have them on the receipted transhaus bills in my pocket, but what did I have to check them against?

Brigit might get to Plagiar's originals.

Brigit . . . or the bully boy.

The bully boy whom I had clipped with his own gun . . . yet who had slipped me Brigit's note . . . he might. . . .

Betrayal.

No matter what you try to do it leads to a betrayal. A betrayal of your own ignorance if Plagiar has already checked the clerk and does not want him.

A betrayal of the lad's whereabouts and an end to the supposed secret you know is keeping you alive, if the prints match.

But you have to know.

You have to know.

CHAPTER EIGHTEEN

The explosion was more a trembling in the ground than a sound in the air, and I felt it, faint though it was, as I was almost at the spaceport perimeter strip.

After the blast came a long, long stillness and slowly, lazily almost, the column of black, greasy-looking smoke began to rise, straight up, into *Poldrogi's* hot, motionless air from somewhere well beyond the low mud-brick buildings that hid the spaceport from my view.

And with the smoke came a rush of people on either side of me and, as I swung onto the perimeter strip itself, from the distance and from nearby on the spaceport tarmac, the red-and-yellow vehicles, all beeping their ear-shattering emergency double-note, high-low, high-low, all streaking toward the rising column of smoke, now beginning to flatten out at the top as that part of it reached and mingled with the high-level thermal layer that turned *Poldrogi's* heat back down onto itself like the lid on a sizzling fryer.

I knew before I reached it what was burning.

The transhaus.

Poldrogi has no department for fighting fires, nor for that matter, had any transit worlds that I'd been on. That dirty job is well taken care of by the spaceport itself, but the police are a local force.

I spoke to a sweaty private in the human line holding back a wavelike swarm of the curious.

"Hurt," I shouted to him over the noise of the fire vehicles, the arriving police, the hoarse bellow of commands, "hurt, is there anyone hurt?"

He did not look at me, he rolled his dark eyes skyward. "Hurt," he said. "A transhaus blows up and he wants to know if there is anyone hurt."

"The clerk," I shouted, and then I recognized the sqaut, red-faced figure of the police corporal in the midst of a small knot of standby police.

"Corporal," I shouted until I caught his attention; after

staring at me a long moment with those cold eyes, he moved close enough for me to speak to him.

"Corporal," I said to him, "the young clerk, Fraan, is he all right?"

He shrugged. "For the moment it would appear that the explosion originated in the manager's office. Whether the boy was in it or not at the time we have as yet no way of knowing."

He flicked his eyes to my wrist. "You are not wearing your timepiece," he said. "It is inside your compartment still?"

I nodded. It was.

"Then I can understand your concern," he said, and he turned his back on me.

He turned his back on me and left me to stare at the back of his red neck under the uniform cap.

The police brass were gathering. I saw captain's bars, lieutenant's, and now even the star of a police general. Did this cool the corporal's ardor for speech ... or was his dealing with me in this manner an idea all his own for solving the two murders he was saddled with?

Or, the thought suddenly struck me, had the corporal his own designs on the wealth, the power, the "everything" Brigit had thought to tempt me with on the dark road behind the Wayfarer's Home?

Brigit.

A motion seen from the corner of my eye and when I looked, there she was, waving frantically to me, almost as she had from the Home parapet before the sniper's shot had whirred past me; waving from behind the police line.

The corporal's back was still to me; I pushed my way to Brigit and when she saw me coming, she at once began to edge out toward the rim of the crowd.

She was by the side of her twin-seated green-and-black skimmer when I caught up with her, her face looking genuinely frightened.

"Anton," she said, and her voice was more a pant than a sounding, "Anton will want to see you. Will you come?"

The note in her voice was new, and it struck me. This was not an order, it was not a wheedling, this was a request. One she obviously felt I might not be willing to agree to.

And what had brought that look of fright to her face?

I indicated the column of now-billowing smoke with my head. "Does he know about this?"

"I don't think so ... I'm sure he doesn't ... it puts a whole new face on things. I *know* he will want to see you ... he *must* see you. Will you come?"

A new face on things. A transhaus blows up and suddenly my importance is so great that for Plagiar to see me, to talk to me is just as suddenly for him a must.

Go with her?

Go with her with so many loose ends, so many suspicions, so many scraps, but no more real knowledge than I'd had when I faced Anton Plagiar before ... ?

I searched my instincts, sought the counsel of the scar on my head, but that had been itching me for so long that, as a guide at this point, it was useless.

I got into the skimmer ... and I didn't know if I'd obeyed a deep-seated impulse ... or had seen and taken into account the black-and-white skimmer I saw coming to a stop near at hand.

Near at hand, but still not close upon us because of the police turning aside of traffic.

But by this time I was getting so that I could recognize Plagiar's blue-and-yellow bully boys at almost any distance.

CHAPTER NINETEEN

We were headed for Plagiar's hostel, that much I could tell from the direction Brigit took. It was not far, I had no time to waste. I plunged, hoping also to make the fear I thought I saw in her face of some advantage to me.

I needed all the edge I could get.

"This has happened before," I said, and the glance Brigit cast back at the pillar of smoke told me that I'd guessed aright.

"Once," she said. "Once before, we thought we were close, and we barely escaped with our lives."

"We?" I said.

"Anton and myself," she said.

"Anton was here just now?" I said, knowing that only moments ago she'd talked as though he hadn't been, that he had to be told of the explosion.

Annoyance diluted the anxiety in her face. "Of course not. You make a great pretense of not knowing things that I am sure you do."

"I'm not pretending that I don't know what this is all about," I said.

"It is enough that you know where the boy is; to know anything more could be dangerous."

"I worry about it," I said. "I worry about things like more money than I can dream of ... and power ... and a dead man only yards from where I am being told of these things."

"Sklar was a fool," she said. "A man well educated and fantastically knowledgeable in the history of thought ... of ideas. But he was a fool."

"He is also dead." I reminded her. "It would be stupid of me to say anything with a second man murdered."

She chewed on that one a little bit. "I can tell you nothing," she finally said.

I reached out and cut the ignition tab; the skimmer dropped to the pavement and chattered to a rough stop. "Good-bye," I said. "I don't plan on talking to Plagiar, or to you, or to anybody else until they let me in out of the cold."

She sat a moment in silence, then reached out a hand toward the tab. I caught it and held it in mine while the silence grew.

I broke it. "I have seen the boy," I said, and for all I knew, I might have.

She turned her head to look at me intently.

I repeated it. "I have seen the boy. I want to know his real identity ... the reason for Anton's offer of fifty thousand Earthside dollars."

The steadiness of her eyes flickered and I could feel her hand in mine go lax with resignation. I let it go and reached for the ignition tab.

I flicked it on. The skimmer rose and now she drove almost dejectedly. And I saw, also, that the stopping had let the bully boys catch up to us.

"Don't take it so hard," I said. "What difference does it make if one more person knows?"

"Anton will kill me," she said, but she wasn't talking to me, she was talking to herself.

"You and Anton know, who else?"

"Sklar, of course, but he is dead."

"Yes," I said. "And so is Mahar Baas."

"You knew. You knew who he really was." And it was not a question.

I knew no more than what the police corporal had told me, but she gave me the credit for knowing the much more that I hoped she would.

"Anton knows, and I know, but Anton has been very careful to keep it from anyone else. He trusts his men to do what he tells them to, he does not trust human nature enough to tell them why."

I nodded but did not speak. She had in her voice that curious blend of relief and secretiveness and she spoke almost half to herself.

She spoke like someone who has kept locked up inside herself a story she was bursting to be rid of, yet one she dared not broach even to the one other person who also knew it.

She was a woman with a bang-up story and she'd had it penned up inside her for too long a time.

I glanced back through the rear window of the tiny skimmer. They were there. At least I saw their black-and-white skimmer close behind us in the light traffic, making no pretense that they were not following us. Plagiar's bully boys.

I looked at the low buildings around us. I did not know the town all that well, but I had the feeling that we should be upon Plagiar's hostel at any moment.

And I hoped that Brigit's story would not take longer in the telling than the time it looked like I had left in which to hear it.

CHAPTER TWENTY

I turned in my skimmer seat to look at Brigit. "You," I said, "have got to be kidding."

She did not take her eyes from the street, the traffic in front of and around us. "It is true," she said. "He was working on a biologically activated locking device, but August Rook worked out a way to transmit matter all the same."

August Rook. The name was strange to me, but the idea of a matter transmitter wasn't. It was on a par with buckets of steam and left-handed wrenches. With the philosopher's stone that was supposed to transmute base metals into gold ... with the universal solvent that could dissolve everything ... except what would you keep *that* in once you'd found it.

No, the idea of transmitting matter was no stranger to me, or to anyone, and I couldn't see Anton Plagiar sucked into anything involving that goldbrick.

Yet Brigit was deadly serious, there could be no mistaking that. But a matter transmitter?

The theory of how one should work was simple enough. For sound, you took a voice, translated it into electrical impulses, and broadcast them. At the desired point you picked up and retranslated the impulses into a fluctuating sound wave which, striking the ear of the listener, gave you the voice effect again.

With an image you did pretty much the same thing except that you dealt now with a pattern of light and shade for the eye rather than a fluctuating sound wave for the ear. And you scanned your image pattern with an electronic pencil at the pickup end ... and used another playing across the face of a cathode-ray tube to retranslate the values it had picked up into an image for the eye to see at the receiving end.

In short, select a point, gauge its value. Transmit your electronic evaluation to a receiver that will reproduce its intensity, its value in exact accordance with your electronic instructions ... and your viewer has his point of light to see.

Repeat and repeat and repeat this gauging at incredible speed and the pattern of light intensities this will produce on your screen will blend and overlap in the eye of your viewer until the image in his mind is one he recognizes as being that of the thing, the person you are televiewing.

The gambit from transmitting an image to transmitting the thing itself is easy . . . and almost inevitable.

For your scanning pencil, select a ray that will not only take note of the surface look of your thing, but be capable of going beneath that surface, of penetrating into your object itself.

X-rays exist; it is only a question of finding one that can be focused to a fine degree, fine enough to scan your object atom by atom.

Atom by atom so that you can analyze and identify each and every atom contained in your object. Analyze and take note not only of its kind and composition, but also of its position within the specific form of your object. This information you, of course, make available to your transmitter in the usual form of electronic impulses to be broadcast.

In your receiver you reverse the process, restoring, each atom in its noted position, each atom of its noted kind, restoring the look, the shape, the composition of your original object.

Simple.

Except that it is a far cry from the simple reading of a light value as reflected from a surface, and the complete and thorough analysis of the atoms that go to make up that same surface.

It is an even further cry to repeating the same analysis for the billions and billions of atoms that lie, not only in that surface, but in the infinite layers beneath it until you have scanned, with your penetrating pencil, every single atom that makes up your object.

Yet Brigit was serious. I could not doubt that.

A confidence game? A deadly serious one if that was what it was. Two men had already died that I knew of. Were there others?

But assume the incredible. Assume that someone named August Rook had indeed found a way not only to analyze an object atom by atom, but, what was even more incredible, more impossible of belief, that he had found a way to transmit this data and *restore* it to a tangible, a touchable, existence. That he could transmit an object. That he could translate a thing into an electronic pattern . . . and then

86

reassemble, from a stock of necessarily unspecified atoms, perhaps even synthesizing the ones not readily at hand, its exact duplicate at any desired point.

And *that* made my mind boggle.

The fact that a transmitter was not necessarily a transmitter alone. It could also be a duplicator . . . and the number of duplicates depended not upon how many objects you were sending, but upon how many receivers you had picking up the signals.

That if you could broadcast a signal, you could also record it. And play back that record again and again and again . . . and make duplicates of the record and thus increase your original object not simply one-to-one, but as close to a geometric progression as you wished to come.

August Rook, looking for a pilferproof lock, had destroyed the need for factories, for whole manufacturing industries, for warehousing facilities . . . even for the fleets of cargo ships that gave the reason for existence to whole worlds, to whole strings of worlds.

Why ship anything if you could reduce its pattern to simple sheets as I did my camera's holograms, and then mail that pattern to its destination . . . at rates that were already notoriously low?

Why make anything more than the one time you needed to make it for a recordable pattern?

Why ship it? Why even buy it when all you needed to possess it was access to its pattern on a bit of tissue-thin plastic.

My mind boggled. Boggled at the thought of a workable matter transmitter, boggled even more at the fantastic, the almost unintelligible, the frightening upheaval that would sweep over the galaxy when the import of its existence was realized.

Control.

And the man who had control of it . . . of its secret, that man would have in his hands a power the magnitude of which had never before been seen, been dreamed of, in all the histories of all the worlds of the galaxy.

The man, it was plain, Anton Plagiar meant to be . . . and the sweat on my face and running down my sides was suddenly cold as the immensity of the stakes he meant to have got through to me.

Stakes the key to which he thought I had.

Stakes Sklar and Baas had died for . . . and a key I knew next to nothing about.

"The boy," I said, surprised to find myself panting a little. "How is the boy involved?"

But we were already at Plagiar's hostel, Brigit slowing to look for her chance to cut across the traffic and into the yawning, flat blackness that was the entrance to its parking area ramp.

Tell me. Before I face Plagiar again, I must know. Tell me about the boy. Tell me about the boy.

The bully boys were close upon us now that we were at their home base. Run? Our skimmer could not outdistance their heavier one.

The street traffic. I saw an opening coming.

"Now," I said. "Now," and our skimmer shot through the small hole in the flow. A small hole, enough to let us dart through, but not enough of a break to let the larger machine behind us do the same.

We swooped down the ramp to the relative darkness at its foot.

"Here," I said, bringing Brigit to a stop in a patch of shadow deeper, to my sun-accustomed eyes, than the general dimness of the underground expanse.

"Down," I said. "Get out and get down behind the cars here, and stay down. Hurry."

She was puzzled and she looked it, but she did drop down out of sight behind the row of parked vehicles I'd pointed to.

The hostel charged better prices than the transhaus; it also gave its guests better service, providing two elevators for them at the far end of the parking area instead of a between-floors ramp.

I darted to the only one of the elevators ready and open. I stepped inside, pushed a button for the topmost floor, and darted out again as the doors started to close.

The empty elevator started its rise, the indicator above its doors slowly blinking off the first of its numbered floor indicators.

I ran back to Brigit and her concealing row of vehicles and dropped down beside her, signaling her to silence.

Time. I'd made it in time. The bully boys came down the ramp with a swoosh, grated to a stop and ran for the second of the elevators even as their skimmer rocked with the roughness of its settling.

They reached its closed doors and the taller one banged out his frustration against them with the flat of his left hand. His right, bandaged and stiff, identified him for me.

88

He shouted something to his companion that I didn't catch, but his meaning was clear enough. With his splinted right hand he was pointing toward the spiral fire-ramp at the end of the elevator wall.

They dashed for it together. At least they started to.

"Hold it."

The voice came from behind me and when, still squatting down, I turned my head, I saw the parking area attendant. A young man in sweat-stained blue coveralls.

And in his hand. . . .

In his hand he held a small stun-gun and he was pointing it not at the bully boys, but at me.

At me crouched beside Brigit and against the row of skimmers he was responsible for.

"Stand up," he was saying. "Easy, very easy."

And as I rose up slowly, facing him, my arms held up over my head so that he could see that my hands were empty, I heard the sound of the bully boys laughing.

CHAPTER TWENTY-ONE

I looked at the bully boys who'd brought me up to his suite. I looked at Brigit who seemed to be interested in a small red mark on the tip of one finger.

Last of all I looked at Anton Plagiar sitting behind a small, very ornate table of native wood I hadn't seen the last time I was here. Before him was a thick sheaf of papers he did not look up from when I was shoved into the room.

He spoke without raising his eyes, his fingers, holding a thin gold pencil, running the lines of the papers swiftly as he did so.

"The explosion. I've had news of it. Was it the boy?"

Brigit answered him.

"It was the same as the last time. There was no chance to see anything."

He pondered that a moment and then he looked up at me, his fingers holding his place on the paper in front of him.

"You," he said.

A tiger. A tiger with the feel about him of an unleashing impatience. A white tiger.

"You. Pike. If you have anything to say, talk."

I took the plunge.

"Anton," I said, calling him by his first name. "I think we ought to be alone."

His eyes, steady on my face, did not move for a long moment. Then they shifted past me and the thin lips under the matching white moustache seemed suddenly to be very easy looking.

I saw the almost imperceptible nod of his head.

Saw the nod and felt at almost the same instant, on my right shoulder, between the tip and my neck, the chopping blow.

Felt the chopping blow and gasped with the unexpectedness of it and the pain.

Pain, hot, intense, flooding my arm and my shoulder, making them tingle with the numb tingle of its paralyzing shock; making me blink with the fullness of its agony.

I was spun, sagging, half around, my hand gripping of itself my aching shoulder. Spun half facing the taller of the bully boys, my face to his patched one split in a grin from one side to the other.

His left hand. He must have chopped down on my shoulder with his left hand, his right still wore the splints and the bandages he'd earned when I broke his fingers with his own gun.

Weak. I felt weak as the pain in my shoulder began to ease ... or was I beginning to pass out from the intensity of it?

I tried to flex my fingers and I couldn't. I shook my head and felt the sweat on my forehead fly.

And I saw the grin grow broader.

Grow broader until there was nothing in my eyes but those teeth and the muscular sweaty throat behind them.

My hand.

My hand that was gripping my shoulder flattened itself and moved.

Flat, it moved ... and edgewise. The short distance from my pain-flooded shoulder to his throat, to the front and a little below where it met the angle of his jaw.

He was lucky.

I was weak ... and it was my left hand. Had it been my right ... and moving with my full strength ... I might have smashed his voicebox.

He was lucky.

Had I known anything at all of what I was doing, my body would have had a practiced pattern in which to move of itself and he would have been a dead man, losing his fight to suck air through the wreck of his throat.

He was lucky. He was only sagged back against the closed door, his eyes popped and straining, his good hand clutching at his throat, his maimed one over it, the splinted fingers stiff, the three still free of bandages wrapped around their mates in a gesture almost pitiful in its futility.

He gagged. He gagged and he retched red and straining ... but he could breathe.

He was lucky.

I was lucky.

I felt his partner's hand heavy on my shoulder, the fingers clawed and pulling.

I was lucky. Lucky that I was hurting too much to be thinking.

"Make it tough," I shouted at Plagiar. "Make it real

91

tough. Fifty thousand? Forget it. I want half. Half of everything . . . or forget it."

His hand with the gold pencil in it shot up. "Dvar," he said and the bully boy with his hand on my shoulder stopped in the middle of his yank at me.

"Dvar. Sit him down, over here." And the bully boy had his arms under mine and was letting me slip down into the broad chair Plagiar had pointed to.

I did not try to hide my sagging. A near-miss from a masher beam and now this to help my strength to come back. I could not have concealed my sagging if I'd tried.

The taller bully boy was leaning against the wall on both his outstretched arms, head down, and the retching sound growing less in his gasping. Neither Plagiar, nor Dvar . . . nor Brigit seemed to be paying him any mind.

Plagiar was handing me a glass. I could not have held it in my right hand, I did not reach for it with my left.

Brigit took it from him and held it up to my lips.

It was smooth, smooth to the point of having almost no feel of its own . . . and it glowed. It glowed warmly all the way down.

Brigit set down the empty glass and now Plagiar waved to his bully boys. Waved them out of the room.

And when they were gone, the one rubbing at his throat and leaning on the other, Plagiar sat looking at me a long, long moment, his fingers drumming on the tabletop.

"It would appear," he finally said, "that you do not take easily to intimidation."

I was rubbing my shoulder; it ached, but not so much that I felt I was going to pass out from it. And I wasn't about to tell him that my beating his bully boy had nothing to do with anything except the sight of that broad, broad grin in the middle of my hurting.

"It helps to bear the pain," I said, "if you know your man won't let himself go all the way."

Brigit cut in, talking to Plagiar. "He knows the boy."

I nodded. "That's right. I know the boy. I don't need his fingerprints or a photograph. I can spot him as soon as I see him."

Plagiar darted a glance at Brigit. "Then it *was* he at the transhaus."

I answered for her. "It was. And the place blew up as before."

I was telling him only what Brigit had told me, but in the

telling, I was hoping that he would give me the natural credit for knowing more than I did.

I didn't feel the ground I was on was any the shakier for the attempt.

Plagiar's grin was suddenly wolfish. "You weaken your position, Pike. You have pointed the boy out to me. Why should I now let you live?"

"You weren't listening, Anton," I said, deliberately using his first name again. "I told you I know the boy on sight. You don't. And the explosions make it clear, to me anyway, that you can't even get close to him without something blowing up. Me, I don't seem to have that problem. I've talked to him, remember."

For the first time I saw that Plagiar seemed to be chewing his lip. "If I could be sure," he finally said. "Sklar was a fool, but a wily one. I have only your word . . . and my reports on him, that I have been following the right boy. He could have deliberately meant to deceive me . . . left a false trail . . . hidden the boy elsewhere."

I had the answer to that one. At least I hoped I did. I used my left hand to take my wallet from my pocket, fish from it the latest of the transhaus receipts.

"If I haven't smeared them," I said, and I was hoping that by saying that I could copper my gamble if I'd reasoned wrong, "there should be a print or two on this that you might find interesting."

I tried to put a note of confidence into my voice . . . but I wasn't sure I'd made it.

Plagiar took the receipt from me, flattened it on the tabletop, pushing aside his papers to do so.

From an inside pocket he took a flat round case about the size of a woman's compact. Opening it, he slid from it a gray, cookielike disk. There was a short handle clipped into the top of the carrying case, but Plagiar did not bother with it.

From his wallet he took a shaded plastic rectangle and slid it under the flat clip that lifted up from the top of the gray cookie.

He slid a tiny lever on the edge of the disk and I heard a faint hum.

Over the receipt he moved the disk, like a man moving a miniature mine detector, and suddenly I saw him and his bully boys, and perhaps even Brigit, doing the same thing to fingerprint records in a Home office while a performance of

93

magic was going on outside to divert the attention of the staff.

Maybe my camera-planted laser hadn't allowed him the time to do the job on *Poldrogi*, but there must have been other places, other times, in which he'd thus searched for the trail of a boy he could know no other way.

The hum changed to a tiny beep and back to a hum again.

Plagiar came back to the edge of the receipt he'd just passed over and the beep returned to stay. It had located for him a latent print that matched the specimen he'd slipped under the clip on its top.

Plagiar put down his print detecting device, and started to get up, not bothering to mask the exultant gleam that had come into his eye.

"It is the boy," he said. "Come, he must not get away again."

I didn't move.

"He isn't there," I said.

Plagiar stared at me blankly for a moment, then he dropped back into his seat. "Of course, the explosion. It masked his escape last time ... he'd be gone before it was set off this time too."

He looked at me speculatively. "And you are gambling your life that I will not risk another such setback, but will make use of your one remaining asset ... that you alone know the boy on sight."

"It is not so large a gamble," I said, "when you consider the stakes. Half of ... of ... ," I groped for a word to describe the magnitude of the thing that the boy could lead him to and I couldn't find one. " ... of the galaxy," I finished.

"You ask a high price for so simple a chore, Pike."

I shrugged. "I was hurting before when I said half. I'm not a pig. I'll take a third."

Plagiar chuckled. The deep-down sound he'd made when the bully boy had put his hand against me and shoved the last time I'd left this room.

"A third. A third of all there is, is not being a pig."

And then he was talking to me. "Pike, I think my promise to give you what you ask would not be believed by you. Why do you bargain?"

It was my turn to laugh. I hope I made it sound real. If I didn't, I had a second hope that he'd figure my shoulder, which I was still hanging on to, hurt as much as ever.

"Anton," I said, "your promise is only a part of what I

want. I know the stakes, and I know the boy. But I don't know how to use the one to get the other. Tell me that and I'll take my chances that you will keep your word."

Plagiar did not need any time at all to figure that one. He held up three fingers, counting them off.

"One, the stakes. Two, the boy. Three, how to use him to get the stakes. I have one and three, you have one and two. I give you three, and you have all the parts to our little puzzle, while I am left with but my original two. And this, you think, will keep me honest."

"That's about it," I said.

I had no illusions about Plagiar's honesty, but I had a very large reason for wanting him to think that I was trying to protect myself on this point and that this was the way I'd figured to do it.

My real motive was much more basic than that. I wanted to keep on breathing.

Somewhere I'd heard it said that he who would ride a tiger must be prepared never to dismount. And that's just where I was. Astride a very large tiger.

Only I'd never chosen to ride it, still didn't know how I'd been euchred into it ... and prize-of-the-galaxy or no, I wanted off.

Being big rich was one thing, being dead rich was another.

My nerves had been beam-shattered, my shoulder judo-chopped. But I was still breathing ... and to keep that up I knew I had to keep this very dangerous man convinced that he couldn't grasp his prize without me.

I heard him sigh. Deeply and loudly. Resignation?

Had Anton Plagiar decided to give in to what I hoped looked to him like the inevitable?

Or was he hoping to con me as I was desperately hoping to con him?

I could not know.

All I could know was that for him the stake was the wealth of a galaxy.

For me, the stake was my life.

CHAPTER TWENTY-TWO

Anton Plagiar had a drink in his hand. My shoulder was letting up its pain and numbness so that I could have held my drink in my right hand if I hadn't chosen to use my left. Brigit was settling herself very decoratively in the smaller of the room's two sofas.

And I knew I had just about as much reason to relax as had that long-ago fellow with the sword hanging over his head. Damocles.

Maybe less. A hair doesn't have a brain, a sensitivity, a whim.

But I hoped my act was convincing ... at any rate, Plagiar was talking.

"I never met Rook," he said. "I have his story from Sklar. Sklar was his friend," and Plagiar laughed when he said that word. "His friend, the man he came to for advice, for help when he was troubled.

"Rook was like so many of our rim-world people, given to much thinking, much brooding, much pondering upon the fact of his existence, much pondering upon the harshness, the poorness of a teacher's life."

A teacher! And I was sure I could have gambled and won that he'd taught on the same planet, at the same school, from which had come Baas and Sklar.

"Something simple," Plagiar said, "something universal, something everyone would need and buy ... that is what it finally drifted into Rook's mind he would need to at least ease the harshness of his life for himself, and for the wife and son he'd tried to settle down to.

"The proverbial better mousetrap was what Rook was after ... and for him it was a pilferproof lock. Small, installed without the bother of the usual wiring, operable only by its own key and no other.

"Bioelectronics was his field of specialization, it was only natural that he stay within it in the thinking out of his lock.

"You know locks, Pike. They have to close when you want

them to and open when you want them to, and not in between. Certainly not to someone else's key . . . and that is what Rook thought he'd hit upon . . . a personal, private key . . . that could not be duplicated by anyone, that was possessed by no one else but the man who'd set the lock."

I could buy that. The man who thought to use a fingerprint believed his key was unique . . . but a photograph could open his lock . . . or a print.

Now a reading of the skin's potential had been added but I knew of a way to overcome that, any photographer did . . . and anyone who didn't mind a stained thumb could open the safebox at the foot of my transhaus bunk.

It was troublesome, of course, but the answer to that was in how big a prize you expected to pilfer. The method was asininely simple. The thumb presented to the lockplate had to have a particular pattern of ridges and whorls. It also had to be living skin to satisfy that part of the key reading.

So, coat the photographic emulsion directly onto the skin of your thumb and print the wanted ridge pattern on it. Now develop and fix your thumb as though it were an ordinary pre-laser, pre-electronic photo, and you have a pattern to be recognized, and the real skin to back it up. The lock is open to you.

Voices, retina patterns, many things had been tried as the operating key to a lock. But hoarseness could blow the one, and a retina-pattern-operated lock had been known too often to ignore an eyeball that was more bloodshot than the one that had closed it.

What had Rook thought of that could be so unique?

"Body cells," Plagiar was saying. "The somatic cells of the body."

Body cells! Bioelectronics, Plagiar had said, was Rook's field. The study of the electronic structure, of the electronic functions of living organisms.

"Soma cells!" I said.

"Yes, the somatic cells of the body. Rook figured, and rightly so, I suppose, that nothing could be more unique to a man than the chromosome pattern of his body cells, and he started with that as his key."

"Lord, to analyze a body cell down to the last speck of its substance," I shook my head at the magnitude of the task.

Plagiar shrugged. "Until we can get his trunk open, who knows how he did it. Maybe he wasn't analyzing the substance at all, maybe he was working on energy patterns, electrical charges. Every man approaches his problem from the position of his own knowledge."

The trunk, I said to myself, remembering the upended service trunk look of the card-producing taboret that Brigit and the bully boy had rolled into the room the last time I'd been here. Plagiar had Rook's trunk. Why didn't he break it open if he wanted what was inside of it? Unless the taboret wasn't masking the trunk ... or there was a good reason, a compelling reason, why he couldn't.

But I had to have the whole of his story. I didn't interrupt him with a question that was so obvious it could be taken as stupid. I nodded my agreement with his sally about the starting point of a man's problem-solving approach and let him talk.

"Rook had a head start on the device he needed to gather the initial cell sample. It was already a part of his work to slice specimens into incredibly thin slices for analysis. He had only to adapt his existing equipment to a shape and a size he could use with his lock."

I restrained the nod I felt myself about to give. I remembered the rubbing sensation at the tip of my finger when I'd placed it on the coin-sized disk atop the taboret. It *had* to be masking Rook's trunk.

"Rook was working for simplicity of installation, with no wiring between the lockplate that picked up and analyzed his cell sample, and the lock that recognized it. So, of course, he used a transmitter on the one, and a receiver on the other.

"According to Sklar, he intended to miniaturize his components when he had his principle worked out; meanwhile he was using whatever came to hand and paying no attention for the moment to its size or weight, which made for a bulky apparatus. And then too, he had to keep his things somewhere safe and separate from the equipment that belonged to the university. . . ."

"So he kept them in a trunk that he could lock," I said.

Plagiar nodded. "Yes; he couldn't work on his lock all the time, he had a living to earn ... and he was getting questions and some poking around from people from whom he was cadging his parts; asking for information he needed that was outside the scope of his own special field." '

"Baas and Sklar," I said.

"Baas, but not Sklar. Sklar was his friend. Rook came to him only after he realized what it was that he had." And again he laughed when he said the word friend.

"He had a working transmitter of matter ... or a duplicator, whichever way you want to look at it," I said.

Plagiar looked at me a long moment before he spoke. "You were not bluffing when you wanted my men out of the room. You really do know what is at stake."

I shrugged, wincing as the motion reminded me of the soreness of my shoulder. "If you didn't think that from the very first, you wouldn't be telling me Rook's story now."

"That is true. And then perhaps it is not. I could be amusing myself by telling you all with the full intention of killing you before you can repeat it to anyone else."

It was a possibility, but I wasn't about to add to the pressure my scar and my brain were already under by giving it to them to consider.

I came as close to a snort as I ever do. "I figure that if it's kicks you want, you've got better ways of getting them," and I could only hope that I was right.

To me, Plagiar's laugh sounded genuine enough, but all the same I was in no position to feel easy about it.

"I have said it before, Pike, you do not take easily to intimidation."

It might look that way to him, but then he didn't have a scar on the top of his head to tell him any different, a scar he was aching to scratch and didn't dare to.

Aloud I said, "Rook didn't know he had a matter transmitter until when?"

"Not until his basic unit was complete and operating ... and he discovered its full usefulness only when he had occasion to test it."

I was remembering that Sklar was an associate in philosophy ... a man would seek out a philosopher friend for help only if he had something on his mind ... something big ... and Plagiar had said that Rook went to Sklar for help.

"And the thought of all that loot in his grasp flipped him?" I said.

"Not just then. You must remember that Rook went to work on his transmitter not for money itself, but for the new life he hoped money would bring him ... and his wife and son. A man with that kind of a mind may find huge sums of money pleasant to think about but that comtemplation doesn't ... how did you put it ... ? doesn't flip him.

"Rook was excited, of course, greatly so, if Sklar was to be believed, but only excited."

"You said he found out what he had only when he tested it."

"Yes. He told Sklar that he had the unit set up and working when it came to him that he'd thought himself right on past any general, any big usefulness, his device might have had.

"You see, he'd wanted a lock that would open to only the one key ... but he'd picked a key so exclusive that only one person in the galaxy could open his lock once it was closed ... and that he had to do personally."

I got Plagiar's point, and I could imagine the dismay that must have poured over Rook when the same thought struck him. A lock with one key ... and one that you had to open personally was fine. But it went too far. You wanted security, but you didn't want to have to drop whatever you were doing to go open a lock whenever someone who had to get past it wanted in.

You wanted a secure key, but one you could hand to someone else, a key you could leave behind if you needed to be elsewhere, a key you could send in your stead ... and you couldn't have it with Rook's lock. It was a great idea, but it had its real and obvious limitations.

"When the thought struck Rook," Plagiar was saying, "he wondered if other things beside a body cell could operate his lock. He had a pencil in his hand ... a metal mechanical one ... he touched it to his pickup button ... and his unit shorted out.

"He tore it apart to find the trouble ... and that was when he found the bits of metal in his lock. Microscopic, but bits of metal.

"He was puzzled. They looked like ... and they checked out to be ... bits from his pencil top ... but he hadn't had it anywhere near the inside mechanism of his lock. ...

"It was then he realized that his receiving unit wasn't just picking up and identifying the pattern of impulses the lock-plate was sending to it ... it was reproducing them also. The body cells he'd sent through it so far hadn't shorted it ... but the first metal bits had."

I don't know if I'd have flipped if I'd had all that potential loot staring me in the face, but Plagiar'd said that Rook hadn't.

"If that didn't flip him," I said, "what did?"

"He was a biologist ... living organisms ... he had to know if he could move something that was alive ... as well as something that wasn't.

"His equipment was getting to be fairly sophisticated ... and the questions were getting to be pretty hard to ignore, according to Sklar. But Rook was eager and he'd found the weak part in his devising.

"His sample-collecting unit. He'd adapted it from a specimen slicer so that what it did in essence was no different from what a meat slicer might do in a packaging plant . . . and while he could hold a bit of metal or plastic in contact with his pickup until it had shaved off as much as he cared to send, he still couldn't do the same thing with anything alive and expect to end up with anything more than a bloody pulp.

"Speed was the answer, Rook felt. A mechanical knife could be made to move only so fast. But a beam of light. . . .

"A beam of light could be made to play over an object so rapidly that the tiny point of its moving could look, to the eye, like a broad flood illuminating the whole of it.

"A cutting beam of light . . . moving at what, for it, was a not impossible speed . . . perhaps it could strip away and scan the whole of an organism in the fraction of its heartbeat."

"It worked," I said.

"It worked," Plagiar said. "On a virus. The first thing that Rook sent that was able to make the trip from his pickup to his receiver was a tobacco mosaic virus. It was a virus . . . but it was alive . . . and the potential of that . . . the moral aspects of it . . . preyed on Rook's mind . . . sent him looking for an answer . . . for help to his friend whose special field was the study of truth . . . of underlying principles . . . of philosophy."

"Sklar," I said.

Plagiar nodded. "Sklar. Rook was looking ahead. Far ahead. He felt that once he'd demonstrated the possibility of transmitting *any* life, it was only a question of application, of engineering, of time, before someone would work out a way to transmit a man. And *that* is the consequence that troubled him . . . the consequence he brooded over. . . ."

It was enough to give any man pause . . . a sensitive man hung on the one horn that meant wealth and power for him and his family . . . a legacy such as no man had ever left before . . . and the second and moral horn that spelled out potential chaos . . . a legacy also such as no man had ever left before, but of anarchy. Hung on these horns, it was not hard to imagine the turmoil that must have been seething in Rook.

Outright murder, wholesale and in unending number, was only part of Rook's dilemma. To analyze his specimen, he had to slice it into its component atoms, destroy it.

With an object it made no moral difference. You destroyed a pencil? You plucked its identical copy from inside your receiver. Or its duplicate repeated end on end until you had all the pencils you could possibly use.

But a man.

Was the man who emerged from your receiver the same man you'd sliced to infinity?

He was?

Then who is the other who is stepping from your second receiving unit? And the third . . . and the fourth?

And remember, if you can transmit an impulse, you can record it.

This bit of plastic magnetized in a directed pattern. You feed it into your adapted receiver and a pencil emerges.

This second bit of plastic. You feed *it* into your adapted receiver . . . and a man steps out.

Is the plastic bit a man? Should you destroy it, are you committing a murder? Or did you already do that when you made upon it the pattern of magnetic impulses?

When you recorded your man.

When you *recorded* your man.

Have you achieved the ultimate depersonalization of a human being?

You have said it before, when you'd taken down a man's name, his service number, his activities, his ancestry even . . . and written them on a card. . . .

You've said that you had him down in your file . . . that he was just a number on a bit of paper. . . . "I have him on my card."

But, of course, everyone, yourself included, knew you were only using an expression . . . speaking an analogy. . . .

But this bit of plastic you now hold in your hand . . . ?

But murder . . . ultimate depersonalization . . . they are only on the rim of the potential.

Chaos.

Two men with an equal and identically valid claim to a piece of property . . . brothers have wrecked each other for what each coveted of the other's possessions.

Covet the other's possession?

Impossible here. How can I covet what is mine own? This other self . . . must I share of my substance with him? And this third . . . and fourth? Lord, there will be nothing left of mine for me.

"Ladies and Gentlemen . . . The President of . . . Mr. President? Mr. President. Which of you is the President. . . ?"

102

"Yes, Ma'am. Three boys all exactly to your pattern . . . delivery? Well, we're a little rushed. . . ."

"Sir, we do not find your attitude at all reasonable. After all, is this or is this not *your* signature?"

"Dear Madam: We deeply regret to inform you of an unfortunate accident. Our equipment is of the finest and rarely does it jam. . . . We realize the burden this places upon you and have already written our Congressman. . . ."

Yes, even a man of small imagination might flip . . . and Rook's imagination was anything but small.

Aloud I said, "It's enough to make any man brood, let alone a man like Rook."

Plagiar shrugged. "There are men . . . and there are men."

I nodded. I couldn't agree more.

Plagiar went on. "At any rate, he went to Sklar for advice to help him make up his mind.

"Of course Sklar didn't believe the fantastic story Rook was trying to tell him, and I suppose Rook wasn't any too coherent about it by now . . . so Rook took Sklar back to his lab to prove to him that he wasn't just hallucinating."

"Sklar believed him, then?"

"Sklar believed him . . . and in his excitement he said things to Rook he told me later he never would have if he'd been able to keep his head. At any rate, he said Rook suddenly started shouting that he'd made up his mind . . . and tried to throw a vial of acid . . . or a thermal cap . . . Sklar wasn't clear what it was except that he knew Rook meant to destroy his transmitter.

"He panicked, he said. He had to stop Rook, and he did. But he said he didn't realize what he'd done until he saw Rook on the lab floor with his head smashed in and he, Sklar, with a heavy glass pestle in his hand.

"There'd been noise . . . and now he heard someone coming. He said his one thought was to hide Rook's body . . . and he did . . . in the only place ready and available to him in the few seconds time he had left."

"In the trunk," I said. "He shoved Rook into his own trunk and slammed it closed."

Plagiar nodded. "Into the trunk with his transmitter, closed the trunk, and slid it the few feet he needed to cover the blood from Rook's head on the floor."

"He made it, then."

"Yes and no. The person he'd heard coming was a lab assistant working late. . . ."

"Baas," I said.

"Baas. Sklar said all he could think of then was to get out of the lab and away. And he did. After all, the trunk was not strange to the lab ... and Sklar was an associate there and known to Baas as a friend of Rook."

"But he went back," I said.

"He went back. He couldn't put the thought of the prize Rook had shown him out of his mind. So he went back, cleaned the floor of blood, and got Baas to help him to his quarters with the trunk, telling him Rook had been called away and had asked him, Sklar, to hold his trunk for him."

I remembered what I'd seen of Sklar and his jumpiness, and I could see a good reason for it. He had his own dilemma goring him with its horns.

Ditch the trunk and you ditch with it all the wealth of the world ... keep it close and you keep close the instrument of your own doom, should it be opened.

"Opened," I said. "Did Sklar get rid of Rook's body?"

Plagiar shook his head. "Rook normally kept his equipment, his notes, everything together in the trunk when he wasn't working on it. When he became upset, he took even greater precautions that his transmitter not be tampered with. Not get out and into other hands while he was making up his mind about it. He not only secured his trunk with his unique lock, but Sklar told me that he'd told him that he'd fitted it with a device that would destroy the trunk and its contents should an attempt be made to open it in a way other than by its own lock. He was not specific, but Sklar believed him. He did not try to open the trunk."

"Then ... then ..." I said, dumbfounded, and pointed with my good arm at the doorway I'd seen Brigit and the bully boy emerge from wheeling a magician's taboret that reminded me of a trunk set up on its end, " ... then you have ... you still have ... ?"

Plagiar looked at me a long moment and then he sighed. "I sincerely would like to know how much you know of yourself and how much you arrive at by observation and guesswork."

He nodded. "Yes, Rook's body is still inside the trunk."

And now I understood Plagiar's impatience too. It didn't make my shoulder feel any the better, but at least I could assign a reason to his testiness.

"But if the trunk is booby-trapped, and Rook's body is inside it ... and the lock is keyed to respond only to his body cells, how. . . ." And my voice trailed off as I contemplated

104

the complete bind that Sklar's moment of panic had put him . . . and Plagiar and, indirectly I suppose, me . . . into.

"But the trunk isn't keyed to Rook's cells," Plagiar said. "He couldn't use his own cells to activate his equipment. He was working with it all the time, touching it, scraping his skin against it, dry cells sloughing off. No, if he'd tried to use his own cells he could never tell if the activating cell came from his touch on the analyzer's button or from a random one that had dropped into the works.

"He had to key his lock to the cells of someone who was not normally in the lab, yet someone available to him now and for the future . . . someone close."

I didn't need him to spell it out for me any further. "His son," I said. "Rook keyed the lock to his son's touch."

And now I had the answer to my why . . . why they wanted a boy so badly that fifty thousand was only an amount flung out impatiently; and why Sklar could lay in a road with his head bashed in . . . and Baas sprawling and laser-lanced in a storeroom.

And my scrape-by with a masher beam was suddenly more than just a memory . . . it was a chilling promise of the future.

CHAPTER TWENTY-THREE

Back to the transhaus I meant to go.

Back to the transhaus and to the one way I could think of to make contact with the boy.

But I meant to go alone. Not with Brigit, and certainly not with either of the two bully boys in the skimmer behind ours, the one bully boy made easy to know by the white flash of his bandaged hand.

"It is of some consequence to me that you not be harmed," Plagiar had said to me. "To provide you with a small escort is the least I can do to ease both our minds."

Ease my mind. . . . I didn't know who'd killed Baas or Sklar . . . and I didn't know and couldn't guess who'd had a try at me with a masher beam . . . so that a bodyguard should have made me feel calmer.

But I couldn't help but wonder about the protectiveness of the bully boy who had a broken hand, a patched-up face . . . and now a granddaddy of an aching throat to bring out his warm regard for me.

And I didn't kid myself that Plagiar's "guards" were anything but a pair of not-too-happy-with-me jailers.

Brigit was driving as usual, and I indicated the skimmer behind ours with a motion of my head. "Your friend who gave me your note," I said, "is he with Plagiar . . . or does he have ideas of his own?"

"I do not understand," Brigit said. But her voice didn't convince me.

"I break a finger for him, yet he slips me your note to meet you out near the Wayfarer's Home. And he does it right under Anton's nose. Why?"

She shrugged. "He is a good friend."

"That may be," I said, "but you don't risk crossing a man like Anton for friendship alone."

She did not change her line. "He is a good friend," but I was rubbing the wrong way from the sound of her voice.

It told me what I needed to know. Any ideas I might have had brewing about enlisting Brigit's help in getting clear of

106

the bully boys behind us I could forget. And to break and run when next she slowed the skimmer down to where I could leap from it without smashing myself up was to make it clear to Plagiar what was in my mind.

And unsuspecting was what I had to keep Anton Plagiar until I'd had my chance to contact the boy ... and to make a clean break ... or at least one that had a more promising start.

"Sklar had a fortune in his hands, and also a body he couldn't dump," I said. "I can see him asking around for a way to exploit the one, but I don't see him blabbing about the other. How did Anton get hold of the trunk? From Baas?"

"No," and she sounded a little relieved. I made a mental note to dig a little deeper, when I got the chance, at the connection between her and Broken-fingers behind me.

"No, Sklar came to Anton himself."

"That is hard to believe," I said. "He knew his murder of Rook would out the moment Anton opened the trunk."

"You do not believe me? Then I can tell you that you have not observed Anton very closely." She paused for a long moment, then added, "Did you know that at one time Anton was a grunt-monkey in an opal mine?"

A grunt-monkey in an opal mine.

That was backbreaking work and as dirty as the name implied. The opal is a peculiar stone, surrounded by superstition and no outfit of size or good sense would take the men or the machines to either synthesize or hunt out the few stones there was a market for.

But although the opal market was small and uncertain, it did exist ... and a man could eke out an existence of sorts digging out the stones.

But heavy mining equipment ... both the shipping or the carrying of it was out of the question ... the opal hunters dug for them with their backs, with their hands ... and it was grunt work in every sense of the word.

Grunt work that killed as many in collapsing mines as died for lack of food, or water, or air, in the harsh regions in which they had to seek the gems.

And Dr. Rolf Sklar, associate in philosophy, had tried to tangle wits with a man who'd survived the opal digs.

But I did not believe that it was Plagiar who'd killed him. The time for Anton to have done that was when he'd first latched onto the trunk.

"I believe that Rook's body in the trunk wouldn't keep

Anton from making capital of whatever else might be in there with it. But I don't believe Sklar would actually look up somebody else to do the opening."

"Tell me, of what use was Rook's device to Sklar? A laboratory model and a handful of notes ... that's all he had. Where were the money, the resources, the technical skills to take the notes and the model and to develop their potential?" Brigit shook her head. "Poor Rolf. He was like a man carrying a soap bubble in a hot wind ... and going out of his mind with the fear of discovery ... and the finding of the right person to do for him what he could not do for himself. And then there was Baas."

Baas. Baas who had helped him carry the trunk to his quarters the night he'd killed Rook.

"Baas knew?" I asked.

"Sklar told Anton that Baas had come to him the next day ... after Rook had not showed up for his classes ... and asked many questions."

"Blackmail," I said.

"Not then, Sklar said. He said Baas just asked many questions about Rook, when he'd seen him last, when he'd been told to take care of the trunk, things like that. Questions Sklar knew would be the ones the police would ask him, and he took it to mean that Baas was being very careful, but that he was letting him know that his presence must be considered. At least that was Sklar's impression then, and Baas made it plainer the next time he came to him. Then he left no room for doubt. He wanted in, but by that time poor Rolf no longer had the trunk."

"Anton had ... acquired it?"

"It was a misunderstanding all around," Brigit said, and she looked over her shoulder, almost as though she were afraid that the bully boys in the skimmer behind us could overhear what she was saying. "Anton meant merely to take advantage of Sklar's presence in his office to make sure that no harm came to the trunk while they were ... negotiating terms."

"You mean that while Anton kept Sklar busy, his bully boys burgled Sklar's place for the trunk." I laughed. "Did Anton know at the time that he ... he took the trunk into protective custody, did he know that it couldn't be opened?"

"Not exactly. I'm afraid Sklar was not entirely open with Anton. He'd told him what was in the trunk, but not that he needed Rook's boy to open it, or that Rook had booby-trapped it."

108

"It must have been a taut moment when Anton found out," I said.

"It was not a good moment for him," Brigit said. "He'd thought to confound Sklar and had the trunk brought in the moment Dvar and Hort arrived with it. He'd expected Sklar to panic, and Rolf did ... but only with fear that Anton would try to open the trunk."

"The boy," I said. "Anton did not try at once for the boy?"

"There was no point to it. It would appear that Sklar had taken the precaution of having Baas take the boy off-planet before he approached Anton."

"Sklar trusted Baas with the boy?"

"It was a small risk that he ran. Baas was an accessory now, and as deeply responsible in the guilt of Rook's slaying as was Sklar himself. And then too, Sklar had the trunk. The boy was of little usefulness without it.

That was true enough, and I could see Sklar, a quiet and philosophical man until his sudden confrontation by the vision of endless wealth and power had brought him to impulsive murder and gutted his life's teachings of any meaning.

"But the boy's mother," I said. "Baas and Sklar surely didn't dare risk the outcry of an outright kidnapping at just that time."

"You do not remember that to August Rook's wife, Sklar was a good friend of her husband's. And Rook had been tense . . . and worried. And that he was a moody man was a secret to no one. Sklar had no difficulty persuading her that it would be best for the lad's sake for him to be sent elsewhere until the worst of what had happened to his father was known. Then too, Baas was no stranger, but someone the boy knew through his association with his father."

I remembered how Plagiar had started to get to his feet and wanted to go after the boy at once when his fingerprint detecting device had found and identified the print on the transhaus receipt I'd given him. He would not have wasted time in taking out after Baas and the boy. I said as much to Brigit.

"It is a large galaxy when you are trying to track down someone," Brigit said. "But Anton is not without his resources. Baas and the boy were not difficult to trace, but we did keep running into one setback after another. Sklar may have been lying to Anton, been fearful of having him catch up with the boy, but he claimed that Baas was not following his instructions as he had given them to him. I think Sklar was as surprised as anyone when a bomb blew out the doors and windows of the room Anton and his men were closing in on, and both Baas and the boy were able to break clear of us."

"But you found the trail again," I said.

"Yes, and now we were careful. Baas seemed desperate for some reason. Had his bomb been better arranged it would have killed anyone who stepped into the room."

And now a second bomb had gone off. But Baas had been dead when this one blew. Had the boy found a new friend . . . or was he now on his own?

With Baas, he had not been able to lose Anton. Without Baas, the boy's chances of escape seemed to have evaporated.

Doubly so, in Anton's mind, now that he had me to spot the boy on sight . . . and the spaceport's routine search-robot stowaway patrol to keep him on-planet.

I had to get away from Brigit and the bully boys for a quarter of an hour, at least . . . and I had to do it in a way that looked natural, that would bring no retaliatory action from Plagiar.

Brigit would not be difficult. I had only to find a rest room with a back door I could slip out of and back in through to be free of her, but the bully boys. . . .

Fifteen minutes free of the one I'd heard Plagiar call Dvar, and his broken-fingered buddy, Hort.

Fifteen minutes free of their seeing me and, more important, of their hearing me . . . and free in a way that would not bring down on me the force of Plagiar's ire.

Fifteen minutes to set myself up with a boy who'd demonstrated, by the blast, an unsettling association with explosives.

CHAPTER TWENTY-FOUR

The transhaus.

We were here, Brigit bringing our skimmer to the grating stop I'd come to expect of her.

And still I had not thought of a way, had come upon no opportunity to grasp, to escape the surveillance of Plagiar's bully boys.

The billowing of smoke was gone, but the bite of it was still strong in the air. Two of the spaceport's brightly yellow fire vehicles were still on guard, their chemical hoses snaking across the walk, up the single broad step, and into the transhaus itself, the revolving door jammed partway open on them.

The police lines were there still, the big brass gone, the crowd thinned, but milling.

The fire hoses piled one atop the other to make it possible for them all to enter the narrow aperture of the transhaus door . . . and the light pressure of my record camera in the pocket on the left sleeve of my jumpsuit. . . . Did I have a way to be free of the bully boys?

"You stay here," I said to Brigit. "I want to get a picture of the crowd to study."

I ducked under the arm of a police private before Brigit could ask what I was about, and darted for the pile of hoses in the doorway.

A picture of the crowd to study. It was standard police procedure to photograph the onlooking crowd at fires for the simple record. Thus later, should evidence of arson be found, the shot could be matched against others taken at similar fires in the hope of finding a face common to all. The one face that had a demonstrably good chance of being that of the arsonist held in thrall at the scene of his crime.

Fraan, the boy, was not likely to be under any such compulsion, but I had the start of my covering excuse.

Onto the piled-up hoses I clambered, being as awkward about it as I dared be. A shout. Behind me I heard a shout and knew it to be from the police private I'd darted around.

I gave it no heed, but turned at the top of the pressed-in pile and fumbled for my camera.

It was up to my eye and filming before I felt hands upon me. I shook myself free, hoping to steam the private.

I made it. His grip on me was firm and there was no getting away from him when I let him pull me down.

"It's nothing," I shouted to Brigit. "They can't hold me. I've got a right to be here." And I saw Dvar and Hort, the bully boys, but their faces were too distant for me to make out how they were taking the police taking me into custody.

"Inside," I said to the private, keeping my voice low. "Take me inside, and find your corporal for me. Hurry."

He eyed me with suspicion plain in his manner.

"Inside," I said, "and get your corporal. Hurry, please."

I think the unexpectedness of the "please" did it. He shoved me up over the pile of hoses and inside the transhaus. I hoped I looked unwilling to whoever was watching me.

The corporal was in the ruins of the manager's office and I saw his head come poking out even as I blinked at the choking, eye-smarting stench. The damage seemed confined mostly to that small room.

"Corporal," I said, "could we hurry? I haven't much time."

"This man," the private beside me had started to say, but the corporal waved him to silence.

"I will take care of it," he said and the private let go of my arm and turned toward the doorway.

"Wait," I said to the corporal. "Could he stay inside for the moment? I don't want someone outside to see him and start to wonder what has become of me."

The corporal nodded to the private and the man stayed. The corporal's eyes were on me. "You said you had little time," he said. "Little time for what?"

I motioned him to come with me as I headed for the down ramp leading to my sleep cubicle.

I came right to the point. "Rolf Sklar and Mahar Baas. I think I can find their killer."

I didn't know if I could. I didn't know if it was one killer or two who had committed the crimes. But I said the one thing that I hoped would hook the corporal.

"You were here when Baas was killed . . . and you found

Sklar on the road ... or so you say. Am I to understand that you wish to confess to both of these murders?"

I broke my stride, but only barely. "Good Lord, no." And the dismay in my voice was so plain that it struck clearly even in my own ears.

The corporal showed me his carved teeth. "My sitting duck has had some hunters let fly at him then ... and he has recognized a face?"

"No," I said. "But I do know things now that I didn't know before, but I need a little clear time."

We were at my sleep cubicle now. I thumbed the lockplate, waited for the ding of recognition and when it came, took out, not my big camera, but my wrist-chrono.

I started to put it into my inside pocket. It hadn't been on my wrist before; I didn't want Plagiar to wonder when or how I'd been able to escape surveillance to come by it.

I started to put it into my pocket, but then I shrugged. I could hide what I meant to do from the corporal, but now he could listen in on me at any time he wished to, might even be monitoring me around the clock. I could not hide my doing of it.

I held the timepiece before my face. "Fraan," I said into it, "this is Eli Pike. You are within range of my voice, that much I am sure of. You are in great danger, that much I think you know. I know why. Repeat. I know why. We must both escape. Repeat. We must both escape."

I was keeping it as matter of fact as I could, gambling the double gamble that it *had* been Mahar Baas who had lightly drugged me and planted the transmitter in my wrist-chrono, and that Fraan, having adopted Baas' technique of blasting when closed in on, would also have taken his receiver with whatever other equipment he had commandeered.

A rendezvous with the boy was what I hoped to arrange, and it did not escape me for a moment, although I was doing pretty good at keeping it out of the front of my mind, that if it had been he who'd blasted the transhaus office, he might very well take me up on a meeting and arrange the same kind of surprise for me when I showed up to keep it.

"Fraan," I said, "we must meet and escape together. Repeat. We must meet and escape together. I will be here," I said, naming as the place, my sleep cubicle for the double reason that it was the only place I was sure both of us knew and that it might have some element of psychological persuasiveness for the boy. He'd escaped from the transhaus once, he might feel he could do it again if I planned a trap.

And also, would Plagiar look first for him right where he'd just run from?

"Do not signal me," I said, fearful that if he tried to acknowledge my call, he might be seen and taken.

"Do not signal me. Twelve hours," I said, making the calculation in my head for a time when we might have the cover of *Poldrogi's* black night. "Twelve hours; I will be here in twelve hours. Until then, do not let yourself be seen. Repeat. Do not let yourself be seen."

"The boy," the corporal said, "he is wanted for interrogation about the fire. I must warn you that my men will be here to pick him up."

I grabbed the sides of my balding head. My timepiece was still in my hand. If he was listening, Fraan would have heard the corporal and there went my chances of his getting in touch with me.

The corporal treated me to a sight of his teeth again. He brought his hand out of his tunic pocket and I saw in it the small gray box of his signal damper, its amber light aglow. "After all," he said, "I did not know what you were about to say or to whom. I could not let you just talk."

I nodded, but he'd cost me precious minutes. "Repeat it," I said. "I must repeat it. And you cannot station your men here or anywhere. The boy will see the change of routine and stay away." I did not mention the chance of them being caught in a bomb blast if that was the way Fraan meant to play it. I wasn't being noble, but I didn't want a bomb safety squad pouring over the building and its subterranean passages to keep the boy at a distance.

"I cannot allow him to go unquestioned," the corporal said. I glanced at my timepiece. How much longer would Brigit and the bully boys stay topside without an edge of action forming on their wondering what had become of me?

"Time," I said to the corporal. "I do not have time. Keep your men away and I will bring the boy to you," I said, and I half believed myself when I said it. "If they are here he surely will not come. If you stay away completely, you at least have the chance that I can bring him to you. It is a small chance against no chance at all."

The corporal chewed on that a moment and I became very conscious of the smarting of my eyes, of the sweat streaming down my sides and dripping from my face.

"Done," he said. "But I must warn you of the risk you

114

take. I will not be easy with you if you are trying to deceive me."

He would not be easy with me . . . *he* would not be easy with me if I had deception in mind.

What would the boy and his explosives do if he had the same idea about me? And what would Plagiar do?

But the amber eye of the corporal's signal damper was no longer burning; he'd turned the unit off.

I brought my timepiece back up to my lips. "Fraan," I said. "This is Eli Pike. I know that you are within range of my voice. . . ."

The *corporal* was going to make trouble for me.

If I'd had the time, I would have laughed.

CHAPTER TWENTY-FIVE

I thumbed the magnification of my viewer to its highest level and hoped that, held up to my eye as it was, it had masked enough of my face to hide my start of surprise from Anton Plagiar, from Brigit, from the bully boys.

There were more of them now in the suite than just the two, Dvar and Hort, I'd taken to be a kind of palace guard. Not as many as had been swarming the Wayfarer's Home, but three pairs of them.

Three pairs that did not even pretend to be doing anything but taking turns at keeping me under constant surveillance.

Twelve hours, I'd told Fraan. Twelve hours. And with the transmitter in my inside pocket, its sensitivity unknown to me, I now had the added strain of keeping outside its pickup area, the voices, the sounds that might nullify my appeal to Fraan, if I was lucky, or lead him to think of me as an enemy that could best be dealt with by a third bomb, if I wasn't.

And I didn't know the limits of the pickup area.

But I did know what my camera shot, taken from atop the pile of hoses in the transhaus doorway, had just shown me.

My taking of the picture had been a subterfuge, something to get me, unsuspiciously, out of sight while I got my time-piece and its transmitter; made my appeal to the boy.

That Fraan would be in it I never would have believed.

But he was, plainly and unmistakably, his antiseptic-looking face, the too-large-looking blond head tilted a little to the side as though he were listening to me instead of looking directly at me, leaping out from the thinning crowd as my viewer went to its highest magnification.

I shook my head. "I don't see him," I lied. "But it was worth taking the shot on the odd chance that he might still have been there, or come back."

And I hoped that the boy, if he were listening, would know that I couldn't have missed him in my shot, know that I was covering for him now; know and be reassured.

Plagiar wasn't being any help to me. "It will be a nice

melon for us to cut up," he said. "Fifty thousand . . . fifty thousand Earthside dollars for the boy." And I knew that he was talking, not for me, but for his bully boys, keeping their sights on simple money, explaining his interest in me in terms that would mask it, but really were only the scratching of the surface potential.

Well, he knew the limits of the trust he could put in his people, or maybe he just didn't trust anyone to withstand so great a temptation.

At any rate, I didn't see that it would make the boy any the more willing to trust me to hear of so large a price on his head.

But I didn't know whether to be heartened or discouraged by the sight of his face in the transhaus crowd. Heartened by the thought that if he had Baas' receiver, he might know of my act about going to sleep and, seeing me being taken inside the transhaus, would listen for a signal.

Discouraged. He didn't have the receiver . . . and if he had, by being topside in the crowd, he was in a good spot not to be listening to it.

There was no help for it. I had to repeat my call . . . and keep repeating it as often as I could . . . and the risk of getting caught at it was just one more thing for me to keep pushed to the back of my mind and out of my thinking.

I coughed. I coughed heavily and, I hoped, convincingly, groping with one hand in my pockets for the packet of tissues I knew I did not have.

My other hand I held over my mouth, mumbling, gasping my apologies even as I pretended to be strangling on my own breath.

Hort, the bully boy I'd given the aching throat to, looked at me with obvious satisfaction for a long moment after Plagiar had waved to him to hand me a drink.

I took it from him. "Tissues," I wheezed. "Do you have a packet of tissues?"

And my gasp was one of relief mingled with satisfaction when Brigit fished one out of her shoulder purse beside her and handed it to me.

"Thank you," I said, brushing it, heavy with her scent, across my mouth, before I put it into my inside pocket.

My inside pocket, the one which also held my wrist-chrono.

Now, if my hands remembered their long-ago skill that Plagiar's use of a magic show to cover his search for the boy had brought back to my mind, I stood what I hoped was a good chance of being able to palm my wrist-chrono and bring it up to my mouth under cover of Brigit's packet of tissues.

Bring it up to my mouth and, from time to time, whisper into it my message to the boy.

Whisper it under the untrusting eyes of Plagiar and his bully boys and hope not to be caught.

And meanwhile, in the next room was a trunk.

A trunk that, if Rolf Sklar was to be believed, had been booby-trapped by a man whose specialty was not in any field that could be expected to give him a familiarity with the trickiness of explosives, but in biology . . . and who, moreover, had rigged his trap while undergoing a mental turmoil that pressed him close to the border of sanity.

I moved my tongue in my cotton-dry mouth, and when I coughed and asked the bully boy for a second drink, my voice came rasping from my throat with a hoarseness that was all its own and none of my doing.

CHAPTER TWENTY-SIX

Outside the windows of Plagiar's suite the moonless *Poldrogi* night was closing in. I saw the reflected glare of crime-lights and once again quieted the unthinking animal urge to simply break and run.

There was another way to be tried first, and the time for it had at long last come.

I stretched in my chair, made a great showing of flexing my cramped neck, arms, shoulders.

The two bully boys Plagiar had left with me were at the alert at once.

I blinked at them. "I don't know about you," I said, "but the clock inside my head says I ought to be asleep. Will one of you call the transhaus for me and see if they're cleaned up enough to let me hit the sack?"

I had expected them to laugh and to tell me that I was going exactly nowhere. Instead, one of them got up and walked to the communicator on Plagiar's table.

He pressed down a tab, spoke into the unit and, in a moment, turned back to me. "Come," he said. "We will take you."

I had all I could do to keep from staring at him. My plan had been unimaginative, but, I hoped, workable. I'd expected a lengthy harangue at the end of which I hoped I'd get across the idea that, if they meant to keep me here, the least they could do was to let me get my gear. Gear that I had to collect personally because it was my thumb alone that could bring a response from the lock of the safebox holding it.

Somewhere, sometime during that escorted trip I hoped, in a way as yet nebulous in my thoughts, but hinging on what chance would present itself to me, to lose my jailers.

Once away, I meant to make straight for the one place I hoped they would not seek me ... the one place I'd been telling them right along I was headed for. The transhaus.

But here were the bully boys, one of them shrugging his shoulders to settle his blue-and-yellow tunic on them, holding open the door for me.

I got a second charge when we reached the parking area

level and stepped from the elevator, the bully boys half a step behind me.

A blatting sound. Twice, and so quickly that I could not locate its direction.

But I heard the bully boys go down behind me. Silently and without even so much as a grunt.

I found myself in the start of a crouch, peering around me, not knowing where to look in the dim overhead lights for the holder of the stun-gun.

And then I saw the movement at the foot of the spiral fire ramp and knew her even before she stepped out from behind the shield of its upright jamb.

"Brigit," I gasped, and could only stare at the weapon she held level in her hand.

"Hurry," she said, dropping it into her purse hung from its strap over her shoulder, "before someone comes." And she gestured in the direction, not of her small two-seated skimmer, but of the larger, heavier, and much faster black-and-white vehicle I'd seen the bully boys using.

My gasp of relief at seeing her put her blaster away was sincere and loud to the point of embarrassment, but still I hung back.

"Whose side are you on?" I wanted to know and was rewarded by an impatient look from Brigit.

"Do not be stupid," she said. "Just how large a share do you think I would get from Anton?"

"And you think I'd be more generous?" I said.

"Since you seem determined to move as swiftly as a rock," she said, "I will put it bluntly. I think you will be easier to cheat. Now get in . . . and hurry."

I clambered into the skimmer beside her, laughing, at what I wasn't sure. Or maybe it was just a senseless reaction to the tension I'd been under these past hours . . . felt no release from even now.

I weighed her sincerity for a split-moment, knew the effort to be useless.

She was looking at me, dark eyebrows up and arched, even as she leaned forward to fire up the skimmer's power plant.

I answered her unspoken "where to."

"The transhaus," I said, and, for no reason at all, thought suddenly of the red mark on her fingertip Brigit had been examining as the bully boys had thrust me into Anton Plagiar's presence, after they'd caught me crouched, with her, behind a row of parked skimmers.

120

The skimmer lifted up, a little heavily I thought, and started to ease out of its parking spot ... and I got my largest charge of all.

Near the top of the ramp, leaning back against the wall, lax as only the young can be, I saw a figure.

He wore stained coveralls and his face was streaked with patches of masking grease, but even at this distance I knew him.

Fraan. The boy Plagiar hunted ... and he was here and not beside my bunk at the transhaus.

I was startled. So startled that I had not the wit or the time to hide my start of astonishment.

But then I caught myself. Why shouldn't he be here? I didn't know the range of the pickup on the transmitter in my wrist-chrono, but it was plain now that the boy had been hearing everything I'd heard or said for something short of a dozen hours.

And it was also plain that he must be aware, by now, that I was the only one who could identify him on sight. And it suddenly struck me to wonder if he was here to make our getting together and away easier, or to safeguard at least the visual aspects of his identity by eliminating me.

Brigit had caught my sudden start of surprise. "What?" she said, and she was peering up toward the head of the ramp. "What is it? What did you see?"

"Nothing," I said. "Nothing at all."

But the boy was erect now and he was not to be missed.

"I see him," she said, her voice suddenly tight and excited. "It is the boy, isn't it?"

My scar was itching, but the impulse in me was strong. Brigit, by blasting my bully boy escort, had thrown her lot in with mine, but she'd also made it impossible for me to go back to Plagiar's suite, to kill time, to wait for another chance to meet with the boy.

It was now, or Lord knew when ... if ever.

"Yes," I said. "Slow it down. Stop. Pick him up."

But Fraan was moving, running lightly and into the street.

And beside me Brigit was shouting. "It is the boy! He is getting away ... stop him ... stop him ... !"

Behind me I sensed a rising and when I turned to look I saw Hort, a stun-gun in his left hand, thrusting up and forward from the floor of the skimmer's back seat. Dvar was already partway out of the open window on his side, his stun-gun emerging from its holster in the singleness of his motion. And I knew why the skimmer had seemed to me to rise heavily at its starting.

The boy was on my side of the skimmer and it was Hort's misfortune that he was too.

"Run," I shouted. "Run, it's a trap."

And even as I was straining my lungs, I was turning in my seat. It was the awkwardest of positions, and I felt in my shoulder the sharp hot sting of stretching tendons as I reached back and out with my arm.

I had no leverage, I had no strength, but with my outstretched fingers I could slap.

And slap I did, across Hort's eyes.

It was a puny gesture, but it was effective ... and it was the one last thing he could not take from me.

He fell back against the seat, both hands up, their backs digging and rubbing at his eyes.

The backs of his hands, because the fingers of one were splinted and rigid, the other gripped and had not dropped his stun-gun.

His gun hand dropped. Dropped enough for me to see the red eye, streaming tears and glaring. The teeth bared in a grimace of fury.

Down came the stun-gun, inches.

Inches only until it pointed full into my face.

I saw it coming, and I tried to duck away, but my arm over the back of my seat, my body twisted, held me.

Dvar, the other bully boy, struck down on Hort's arm, but the gun went off all the same.

At this close range, even the cushioning of the seat back could not save me entirely.

I felt the numbness strike and my body begin its senseless slumping down.

I'd been told that to be hit by a stun-gun bolt was not particularly painful ... but that man had either never been hit or was a liar.

I was numb, all right, but I also ached all over. And I almost welcomed the blackness that was nudging itself mushily into my brain, even though its coming would leave me not knowing if my distracting swipe at Hort had given Fraan the extra split-moment he needed to make his breakaway good.

CHAPTER TWENTY-SEVEN

Tingles.

Tingles. Tiny, sharp, aching, like that of a leg that has fallen asleep and is now awakening.

But this leg is all up and down my body, both sides, my arms out to my fingertips.

My scalp. Even in my scalp I can feel the tiny needles prickling.

I tried to move my head and the swelling of the needles at my attempted motion brought the streaks of red to a bursting at the back of my eyeballs.

Red. Red in my eyes and Brigit's face peering down at me.

Red mark on her fingertip.

Red mark like a little half moon ... on her fingertip ... and the bully boys shoving me into a room.

And even my fuzzing brain knew the answer to that.

Brigit, crouched down behind a skimmer, her arm up to the partition close behind her, her finger pressing hard on a button.

The button that was meant to summon the parking area attendant from wherever he might be ... the button that would leave its half-moon mark on her finger from the hardness of her pressing.

It had been no accident then that I had been come upon from behind by the attendant with a stun-gun in his hand ... come upon and delivered to Plagiar's laughing bully boys.

And if it was Brigit who'd betrayed me then, was it Brigit who'd betrayed me now?

"Lied," I said, and my tongue was thick and it tingled as I forced myself to move it. "Lied, you lied to me."

The face peering down into mine smiled. "I asked what you thought my share would be and then I told you you would be easy to cheat ... were these lies?"

"Lies," I said. "Lies," and it was floating out of my mind why my tongue should be saying that word of itself.

I heard a man laughing. "A little more time. They all come out of it feeling put upon."

Put upon. . . .

I had been masher-beam grazed, riot-dyed, judo-chopped . . . and now stun-blasted.

I had been lied to, chased by a lynch mob, and sucked into the treasure hunt of the ages for a reason I still did not know.

I knew I was suspect in two killings and would be in a third if Rook's trunk was ever opened without it blasting away a city acre.

Put upon. Some ape was laughing because I was coming awake feeling put upon.

"He is grating his teeth," I heard Brigit say.

"That is normal," said the man's voice and now I knew it to be that of Anton Plagiar. "It has something to do with the body storing up its frustrations during the time it cannot move freely, I think."

I *was* grating my teeth. And now I deliberately forced the knots at the sides of my jaws to loosen, tried to let my body fall limp and loose so that the ache and the tingling would let up.

"Get him up on his feet," I heard Plagiar say. "Walk him around, I don't want the discoloration to form."

I felt hands tugging at me, lifting me up, and I could do nothing except go with them.

Discoloration. The same man who'd said a stun-bolt didn't hurt had also said that exercise, begun as soon as possible after control is regained, and kept up until the breathing is heavy and the heart pounding, would help prevent an aftereffect that otherwise leaves the body looking as though it had been lightly bruised over its entire surface.

He'd been a liar about the pain, he could be a liar about this. I wanted down . . . sit . . . lie down . . . anything to ease the crescendo of needles that each movement the hands gripping me compelled me to go through.

"He is sweating," someone said.

"Good," said Plagiar's voice. "He is over the worst of it."

And with the first pouring of sweat I realized that even in *Poldrogi's* heat, my skin, up to this moment, had been dry and powdered feeling.

"I'm all right," I said, and now I could feel that the hands gripping me had to use their strength to keep me from

124

jerking myself free to stand glaring at Plagiar and the others in the room.

The others. Brigit. Dvar. Hort. The two bully boys Brigit had blasted.

The two bully boys Brigit had blasted!

The two of them, standing there, grinning at me. Neither of them looking in the least as though they'd just gotten over what I was going through.

They caught my wide-mouthed gape and their grins grew broader. Plagiar laughed. "Surely you did not think that Brigit actually blasted my men did you?"

I closed my mouth. "No," I mumbled. "No, I suppose not."

And it was beginning to soak into my addled brain that Plagiar was not being solicitous for my welfare when he'd order his men to keep the bruise effect from forming on my body. A man who wished to avoid police attention enough to have his bodyguards use riot weapons in subduing a possible assassin, as had the man who'd dye-stained me on the platform, would also not want stun-bruises to be in evidence to spark questions.

And Plagiar didn't need me now that Brigit and maybe two of his bully boys had seen Fraan.

Now that my head was clearing I sensed about Plagiar, about Brigit, a certain air of waiting. Even Dvar and Hort seemed to have it and I had a sudden hope.

A hope that the boy, with his masking of grease and coveralls, was not recognizable ... had made it safely out of sight and away.

Plagiar chilled the hope almost at once. The communicator on his table rang lightly and he lifted up a tiny earpiece before he flipped a tab.

He nodded. "Fine," he said. "And cautiously now. We do not want to startle him into running again. And do not let your taking him be seen, do you understand?"

He nodded again, said "Fine" several times more before he flipped the tab off again and put down his earpiece.

He did not have to spell it out for me. His men could not very well pounce upon their victim and wrestle him to the ground. Not in the full glare of a city's crime-lights, not on a strange world where they were at best but visitors.

Not if they were Plagiar's men and practiced in unobtrusive action.

The boy was still at large, but from the look of Plagiar's face it was now only a matter of minutes.

So few that even now Brigit was leaving with Hort, and I knew that when they came back into the room they would be wheeling Rook's disguised trunk before them.

I had a hope left, a double one, hinging on the transmitter hidden in my wrist-chrono in my pocket.

The boy, from what Plagiar had said into his communicator, was not running now. Might even think that he had lost his pursuers. If I could but bring my timepiece up to my mouth and speak into it secretly again, I might still warn him of his imminent capture . . . might still help him evade it.

And the police corporal had told me that his people had broken the scrambled signal the transmitter was sending and that he would be monitoring it. If I could at the same time summon him, he might arrive in time to catch Plagiar with Rook's trunk . . . and his dead body . . . or at least get here in time to save my neck from whatever Plagiar had planned for it once he was sure he had the boy.

The pressure of Brigit's packet of tissues was light in my pocket and I coughed and started to reach for it.

I coughed and I started to reach, but stopped in mid-motion.

Plagiar was grinning at me and, dangling from his finger, pulled at that moment from its concealment in the pile of papers on his table in front of him, was my wrist-chrono.

My mouth was suddenly rasping dry.

"When?" I croaked, "when . . . did . . . you . . . ?"

"When did I first suspect what it was you were doing . . . or when did I take your chrono from you?"

"When?" I said, and my voice was no stronger, no clearer.

Plagiar laughed. "I took it from you when you were unconscious, of course."

He turned my timepiece over and I saw that its back was open, the transmitter presumably gone. He had perhaps thought to cut my link with the corporal and my one hope of help.

"I suspected what you were doing," Plagiar said, "when I noticed a certain arching to your hand when you had it up to your face."

He let my timepiece drop back onto the table, his eyes looking vastly amused, his manner expansive.

Expansive. I supposed I would feel expansive too, if I thought I had in my grasp what Plagiar thought he was about to have in his.

He was talking, " . . . the palming of an object does have

126

about it a look recognizable to the knowing eye. Surely, Pike, as one dabbler in magic to another, you did not really have more than a forlorn hope that your little subterfuge would go undetected."

I did not answer him. I could not answer him. He had seen what I was about and he had used it, and me, to bring to him the key he needed, had hunted, to realize his fortune.

The fortune the true proportions of which he did not trust his men to know and, knowing, retain their loyalty to him.

But Plagiar knew the true potential.

Brigit knew the true potential.

And I knew.

From a drawer in his table Anton Plagiar was taking a flat handgun oddly shaped; one with the double-barreled look of a slim pencil-sized tube projecting from inside a larger, stumpier outer one.

A laser weapon . . . the kind that had killed Mahar Baas.

My hope for the boy's escape was gone. For myself there was suddenly the racing of my heart and the breathy, top-of-the-lungs feeling of naked danger.

CHAPTER TWENTY-EIGHT

They were wheeling the trunk, in its taboret disguise, into the room; Hort pushing it, Brigit close behind him.

Plagiar sat at his table, his laser pistol, the safety off, lying at the ready in front of him ... and I knew what he was saving me for.

The trunk. Not even Dvar and Hort, the men who had stolen it for him from Sklar, knew fully what was in it. And when the boy was brought in and the time came for it to be opened, I was sure that he meant to have in the room only the people who shared its secret with him.

Brigit ... and myself.

And I did not need to wonder to whom Plagiar intended to delegate the not-pleasant-to-think-about chore of actually and physically breaking open its closed sides.

"How long," I said, intending to ask how long Rook had been in it, but aloud I said, "how long have you been hunting the boy?"

"Months," Plagiar said. "Months."

And his avid stare was on the trunk, leaving me to contemplate for myself what would hit me when, under his gun, I would shove open the trunk and begin to strip it of its secret.

Left me to contemplate the thought that, afterward, there would be no appreciably greater difficulty getting rid of the stripped trunk if, in addition to Rook's, it held a second body. Mine.

The trunk was in the room, on the wheeled base, its sides draped with the magic-symbol-covered hanging, the coin-sized disk set down into what was intended to, and did, look like the top of a magician's taboret.

Plagiar's laser pistol, the safety off, was very prominent in my eyes.

"All right," he said, using his left hand to gesture at the two bully boys whom Brigit had pretended to blast in the parking area below. "Dvar and Hort can handle it, you two go."

And when the two men had gone, he spoke to Hort. "Strip it," he said, indicating the trunk. "Remove that magic nonsense."

Perhaps I was jumpy, my nerves stretched taut to the point where I could almost hear their twang inside my head, but I had the feeling that Hort hesitated before he walked to the taboret and started to rip away at the hangings.

"The top," Plagiar said, "lift off the top and the rest will come with it."

Hort had ripped the hangings up the front and now he tilted the top up and back and started to slide it free of the trunk top.

I now saw that the disk was flush with the trunk surface and the top connected to it in no way.

"The card production," I said, "it has no connection with the disk at all."

Plagiar laughed. "How could it?" And then to Hort, "Bring it here."

But Hort had already thrust a finger of his good hand through the hole in the taboret top he had standing on its edge and, in a moment, the slender wand with the card on its tip popped out. It was still the trey of diamonds.

"A completely separate arrangement," Plagiar said, "and it allowed me to keep the real device available at an instant's notice." He sounded and looked satisfied to the point of smugness.

His communicator gave its genteel ding and he was at it instantly, the earpiece to his ear.

When he put it down, I did not need to hear the words to know what he was about to say.

"They have the boy. They are on the way."

And if he had been on his feet I was sure that he would have danced a jig. As it was, he leaned back and rubbed his palms together.

Rubbed his palms together, his head thrown back, his breathing heavy.

The pistol in front of him. Leap for it now?

And then I saw the turn of Hort's head to look at Brigit, saw her nod, saw the fat-barreled, carbine-length weapon come up from its concealment in the taboret hangings Hort had handled so awkwardly.

I heard its masher beam whir once . . . in the direction of Plagiar. And then Hort had snapped it to his right, fired again, and was back to cover Plagiar.

I heard the dead fall of the body and I did not have to

look to know that Dvar could literally not have had the time to know what hit him.

Plagiar had snatched up his pistol and was firing it at Hort.

At least his hand was moving in that curious pumping action of a man pulling a trigger again and again ... but nothing was happening except that as his hand pumped he seemed to be having trouble keeping his arm up; staying in his seat.

The masher beam. Its peripheral shock wave had struck him and now his nerves were feeling the same shock effect as had mine when I'd been hit on his dipping and pitching platform.

Hort stood his ground behind the trunk, his sniper's carbine pointing easily at Plagiar, snaking between him and me ... and I knew who it was who'd fired the shot at me at the Wayfarer's Home.

Who it was that had been beside Brigit on the roof, dropped down out of sight behind the parapet, not betrayed by her because she did not want me, hiding in the bushes, to know, but because she really had intended for me to kill Anton ... and be dropped myself in the next instant. It was Anton who must not know of Hort.

And seeing me bring my camera up to the ready she could think only that I was taking the Anton-double to be the real man and meant to shoot without waiting for her signal.

Stop me, she had tried, with her frantic waving, and it was only the habit of my hands, checking my camera for the strangeness of its feel, that had triggered the killer laser prematurely.

The killer laser that Hort had slipped into it in the brief moment it had been out of my hands and sitting beside Brigit's purse on the table outside the Home study.

I knew all these things ... and did I also know who, guarding Brigit during her meeting with me in the blackness hard by the Wayfarer's Home, a meeting he had helped arrange by slipping me her note, had bashed in Rolf Sklar's head when he had come upon him moving up on us in the dark?

It was Brigit who spoke. "You might live a little longer, Anton, if you will sit back and stop trying to fire that silly pistol of yours. It will not work."

It wouldn't. Hort had fired his carbine, not at Plagiar, but at the pistol on his table. A near miss would have been enough. Its emmiting crystal was fairly sturdy and might

130

survive, but the envelopes of its twinned light-source tubes were wine-glass thin and could not, and did not, withstand the vibration of the beam's brushing touch.

Anton clutched at the edge of his table, fighting to stay upright, and I wondered if my face had been as sick-looking as his was now.

But I did not dwell on the thought. Hort's carbine, snaking between me and Plagiar, suddenly came to rest on me alone.

"Do we need him?" he said over his shoulder to Brigit.

She laughed. "We don't if you do not mind opening the trunk yourself when the boy gets here." She indicated the trembling Plagiar with a tilt of her head. "Anton will be no help."

Hort studied me for a long moment before he shot a glance at the trunk.

"I think I know what you mean," he said, and he laughed.

And it wasn't until I let it out in a noisy gasp that I realized I'd been holding my breath.

Holding my breath and trying hard not to see the broken fingers I'd given him, the face patches ... trying hard not to think of the chop across his throat ... of the slap across his eyes.

Trying hard and not making it.

CHAPTER TWENTY-NINE

Plagiar had moved over to the larger of the room's two sofas. He sat back in one corner, his feet up and crossed, his arms tight against his chest and stomach. From the look of his face I judged that he was getting as used to the ebb and flow of his strength, the phasing feeling of it, as I had when Hort's sniper beam had whirred past me.

"You want it all ... and you want me dead," Plagiar said, and he sounded as though he could not believe the words.

Brigit did not bother to smile. "I take from you no more than you tried to take from Rolf Sklar," she said. "If you had not leaped upon him at once and taken his trunk, he would have had Baas come back with the boy from wherever they were hiding and all would have been well. He would not have had a reason to approach me, to persuade me to join forces with him so that between us we could cope with what he could not handle alone ... your greed."

Persuade her. I wondered just how hard a job Sklar had had doing that ... and would he be alive now if he hadn't succeeded?

"You want me dead," Plagiar said again, still sounding as though he couldn't believe it.

He raised his eyes to me. "Then you were working for her and not on behalf of the boy when you tried to kill me with the weapon in your camera."

So that was why he had covered for me with the police, removing the laser, restoring my camera. Thinking that, working for the boy, if I were free I would lead him to him.

Well, in spite of my ignorance, I had.

I looked at Brigit. "Why me?" I said, remembering what she had told me in her skimmer. "Sklar didn't give you my name ... tell you where to find me. He couldn't have."

The puzzlement in her eyes looked genuine. "But he did," she said. "At first, when he told me you were an innocent he had found for us to sacrifice so that we could dispose of Anton with no risk to ourselves, I believed him. But then when I saw him offering you all the money he had, I knew

132

he'd lied to me ... that you really were working with Baas and knew where the boy was. That he'd found you and was hoping, through me, to get rid of two obstacles ... you and Anton ... at the same time."

Not *all* his money, I said to myself, remembering my quick glimpse of the figures on the sight-draft he'd pushed toward me in the gasthaus, not all his money.

And I wondered if Sklar really thought I was with Baas and had tried to kill me as Brigit had just suggested ... or did he come to me in full sight of all to drag me like a red herring across some unknown trail of his own?

"You are a false woman," Plagiar said to Brigit; then he looked up at Hort, standing over him, his carbine held loosely in the crook of his arm. "Do not trust her as I did," he said. "She will get to you when she is ready. She wants it all."

Hort grinned at him. "You cannot get me at her throat," he said. "We will not fall out." And he nudged the fallen body of Dvar with his toe. "She knows that if I hang, she hangs with me. It is as simple as that."

Brigit might have been joking, but she sounded genuinely hurt. "Hort," she said, "you wouldn't."

He spread his grin to include her in it with Plagiar. "Do not put me to the test, loved one. Do not put me to the test."

The communicator on Plagiar's table dinged and suddenly the color was high in Brigit's cheeks and her eyes glittered.

She reached over Plagiar to take the carbine from Hort's hand, prodded Plagiar with it.

"Answer them," she said. "Answer them and tell them Hort will be down for the boy. Tell them to return to their stations, that you will need them no more tonight. And Anton ... do not be stupid and try to say more."

She stood over him, the carbine pressed against his skull as he spoke. And when he was through she stepped back and motioned him back to the sofa and away from the communicator.

Her finger was inside the trigger guard of the carbine, its barrel upright now, the curved butt resting on one hip. She handled the weapon with a practiced ease that killed any thought I might have had of jumping her once Hort was out of the room even as it was being born.

And the sight of Plagiar's pistol, lying on the tabletop where he'd let it fall from his phasing fingers, was made doubly galling for me by my knowing that it would not fire.

"Bring the boy up," she said to Hort. "And be sure that you return alone."

"They will not know," Hort said. "They will not suspect." And he was gone, leaving me under Brigit's eyes and the unnatural glitter that was rising in them.

The silence grew until all I could hear to break it was the heavy rasping that was the sound of my own breathing, the low retch that was Plagiar at the turning of a phase, and now . . . as I strained to hear Hort's returning with the boy . . . a faintly blubbering sound that I did not place until I saw that it seemed to be keeping pace with the rise and fall of Brigit's breathing through her parted lips.

CHAPTER THIRTY

Sounds.

Sounds of the elevator, opening and closing.

Footsteps.

Sounds of doors being opened, and closed, and locked again.

Sounds to raise the strain of listening to Brigit's breathing growing tighter, seeing the quiver of the carbine's upraised tip increase, the glitter of her eyes grow glassy.

And then Hort was in the room, thrusting the boy in before him.

The boy who moved easily, unresistingly almost, in his stained coveralls, and who did not lose his balance at Hort's forceful pushing.

The boy who now stood as erect as I remembered him in the transhaus corridor when he'd led us to the body of Mahar Baas.

Erect, and on his face a calm that even the streaks of grease with which he'd tried to mask himself could not completely hide.

"I'm sorry, Fraan," I said. "I did not mean for you to be caught."

His eyes, moving toward me, and his voice were as calm as his face. "You are a friend," he said, and to me he sounded as though he was saying it more to identify me for himself than as if he meant it to be a comfort to me.

The upraised tip of the carbine was shaking visibly and Brigit handed the weapon back to Hort.

"Watch them," she said, and she took hold of the boy's wrist.

He did not move, and she tugged at his arm. "Come," she said, and again, "come."

Hort prodded him with the tip of the carbine and the boy looked at it and at him with no change of expression that I could see.

But he moved.

He moved to the side of the trunk and let Brigit lift up his hand to the disk set into its top.

Laughter. Retching, weak laughter, but laughter.

I swung on Plagiar. So did Hort with his carbine.

Brigit stopped in mid-motion, the boy's finger extended in the grip of her hand, the tip of it pointed toward the disk on the trunk.

Plagiar laughing. "It would be funny," he gasped, with his weakening-phase lungs. "It would be oh so funny if Pike has led us to the wrong boy."

"You are a fool," Brigit spat at him. "You checked his fingerprints yourself."

And she thrust Fraan's hand down the remaining scant inch it had been hovering over the disk.

Thrust it down and held it.

Nothing.

Nothing happened.

No whine of equipment activating, no click of a holding latch snapping back.

Nothing.

The thought of grease from his coveralls or his face coating his finger occurred to her as it occurred to me.

She lifted up Fraan's finger from the disk, wiped it angrily with her skirt, the blubbering sound of her breathing growing loud enough now to be heard without straining.

Back to the disk she moved the boy's hand, he all the while watching her do so with as much interest as might be displayed by a huge doll.

Shock, I thought to myself. The boy is in a state of shock that borders on the catatonic.

And now she had his finger back to the disk, pressing it down until it bent back at the joint of its tip, her own growing white with the force of her gripping.

And still nothing.

She fell back, bewilderment on her face, and the boy stayed as he had been put, his finger still on the disk.

And now Brigit was staring into his face, the blubbering a heave, her eyes almost on stalks with the intensity of her looking.

And she screamed.

A scream of rage that opened her mouth wide and brought flecks of foam to its corners.

She screamed and she clawed at the boy's eyes.

She clawed and even Hort took a step forward before he saw what she was about.

She clawed, but only at the boy's left eye, at the eyebrow above it; he not bringing up an arm to stop her.

136

She clawed and I felt the start of a shudder as I saw the skin come away in a clinging strip.

But it was only the start of a shudder, stopped when I saw no blood, saw only the faintly-lilac-glowing "A."

An android.

Fraan was an android and, as such, of course could not operate any cell-keyed lock, and of course he would have the real Fraan's fingerprints.

He would have the fingerprints of anybody you chose to make a cast of for a pattern, and Baas had managed the time for it least that much.

I laughed. Laughed without my really being able to help it. Laughed because I suddenly remembered something that the police corporal had told me about Baas.

That when he had disappeared from his university's lab there had gone with him equipment that his employers did not wish to talk about.

A bio lab . . . a bioelectronic device.

An android, or at least the makings of one. And of course they would not wish such laxness in security to be known, at least not until that valuable property was safely back under wraps again.

Mahar Baas.

Mahar Baas was not the blackmailer coming to him for what he could get that Rolf Sklar had taken him to be; a tool to be used to keep key and trunk apart until Plagiar could be contained or killed. Mahar Baas was, instead, the friend of August Rook who realized that he had been duped into helping another steal the fruits of Rook's work.

The friend who perhaps sought to recover those fruits for Rook's son . . . or at least to confirm his suspicions as to Rook's fate . . . but who Sklar alerted to the real danger when he spoke to him of Plagiar and the need for getting the boy safely out of reach.

The friend who stole from the bio lab that he worked in with the boy's father the android he needed to be the wild goose in the chase he meant to lead them all.

His trail, hidden enough to keep his pursuers unsuspecting, yet open enough for them to follow him while he led them away from their real prey. Acting exactly as Sklar had told him to, except in one respect, in one all-important respect.

Brigit caught the thought as quickly as I did.

"Baas!" she shrieked. "Baas! He never took him away at all. The boy is still with his mother."

Hort. He was goggling at Brigit, the masher-beam carbine sagging.

Now. Leap upon him now!

But even as I started the move he caught it and for me to complete it meant only to throw myself directly into the beam of the carbine coming up.

But I had started to move. I could not stop now. I could only change direction.

To the side I went. To the side and over the top of Plagiar's table, tipping it over with me.

Over and down, in a flurry of flying papers, of crashing sound, of a sliding, wrecked pistol, to crouch behind the puny shelter of the upended top.

"Kill him." Brigit shrieking. "Kill him. Kill him."

"Gladly," I heard Hort say. "But not with this. Not quickly. Not easily. I owe him too much to do him that favor."

I spun around to dart a quick look over the top of the table edge before I dropped down again.

Hort had handed his carbine to Brigit and my quick glimpse had shown me him beginning to remove his blue-and-yellow tunic. It was plain he meant to pay me back for the broken fingers, the mashed face, the simple indignity of his having to take them.

And beyond <u>him</u> was the hot-eyed, wild-eyed Brigit with the carbine poised.

I pounded the floor with my fist, danger and frustration choking me ... and then I saw Plagiar's pistol ... and felt the flail of my record camera in the sleeve pocket of my jumpsuit.

I snatched up the wrecked pistol, pressed on its hooded top, struggling for a breath-holding moment with its refusal to budge.

The masher beam, if its vibration had disturbed the molecules of the metal, of what use ... ?

The top snapped open and the gun almost flew out of my hands.

I caught at it, peered inside, swearing at the sweat that wanted to have me killed by pouring down into my eyes at just this moment.

I peered and I saw that I was right. The long crystal that emitted the invisible rays that made of this laser a killing weapon was intact, but the bits of broken glass demonstrated that the tubes that were the source of exciting light had indeed not withstood the vibration's touch. Their tiny foil reflectors sagged at my touch.

I put the pistol on the floor and snatched at my sleeve pocket and my record camera in it.

The windows in front of the flashtubes that provided the light for its pictures gave me no trouble. No trouble at all, and I threw them aside and reached for the tiny flashtubes they were meant to protect.

"You, behind there. Pike. Do you hear me?"

It was Hort, ready for me now, ready and limbering, and having his fun making me sweat.

Well, sweating I was. Sweating and my fingers slippery with it, and the glass surface of the tiny flashtube they probed at slick.

But I had it free of its clip.

And now I had its mate too.

The pistol.

Could I make them fit the pistol?

Short. They are a little too short to reach from terminal to terminal.

"Pike. Come out and I promise to kick you only when you are down."

And he was laughing. But now I heard him moving toward me.

Clips. Bend the pistol's clips to reach.

How?

Don't have the leverage with my fingers alone . . . have no tool.

Foil. Foil reflectors can conduct current. Slide them. Press them down and slide them a little to make them reach.

No. Too light. Will not stand the current. Blow out with first shot.

Nothing else. Hort close upon you.

Nothing else.

May not need more than the one shot.

One shot.

All it takes is but one shot to prove a gun works.

I slid the tiny foil scraps endwise, creasing them to make contacts for my flashtubes with the pistol's clips. I slammed shut the hooded top, came up over the edge of the table with the pistol in my hand and pointing.

Pointing.

And even a pistol that you know does not work will make you stop in your tracks, if only for a moment.

Hort stopped.

And then he laughed and moved forward. And I pulled the pistol's trigger.

I fired it.

I fired it, but not at Hort.

I fired it at Brigit.

Brigit who was bringing her masher carbine to a line on me.

Brigit who dropped the weapon and spun back, clutching at her side.

The left. The vibration has shifted the lenses to throw to the left.

Hort was frozen in his tracks, staring not at me, but at the weapon he thought to be dead come to life in my hand.

I kept him that way.

Kept him frozen in his tracks with it and at the same time spoke to Plagiar.

To Plagiar who, sitting back in the corner of his sofa, had about him a waiting air that I knew from my own experience meant that he was waiting for a stronger point in his phasing strength before making a leap for the carbine lying on the floor.

"Don't you try it," I said. And inched over until I could feel it under my hand.

Only after I had picked it up did I let my eyes lessen their darting from Plagiar, sullen in his corner, and Hort, now recovered and watching me.

And Brigit. Eyes hot with anger and pain. Holding her side, sagged down on the floor where her seared side had dropped her.

"Back," I said to Hort, making the motion with the carbine. "Back."

And when he was clear of the tipped table I snaked toward it sideways and hooked the cord of the fallen communicator with one foot.

I did not duck down behind the table, nor did I take my eyes from the three in front of me.

I pulled on the cord with my foot until the communicator was out in sight. Then I squatted down beside it, pressed the tab carrying the hostel's own symbol and, when the genteel voice answered, asked for the police.

He was a good hostel man. He would have stalled until his own security people could come up and have a try at keeping any matter calling for police attention quiet.

I cut him short. "The city police. Anyone else comes through the door gets a masher-beam bolt in the stomach."

"Yessir," he said, hurriedly. "Yessir, the city police." And I could hear the sound of his fumbling with the connections.

140

I turned to the android. "Fraan," I said, "can you hold this weapon on these people for me?"

I was afraid that I knew the answer, but I had to ask the question. There was something that needed to be done and before the police got here.

Androids do only what they are programmed to do, so the one I'd called Fraan did not shake his head.

"No," it simply said. "I am programmed only for evasion and the leaving of a trail."

And the answer told me that, while the first explosion Brigit had told me of might have been set off by Baas, the second was the work of the android, following a preset plan that had successfully covered their escape before.

But with Baas dead, there was no one to give it new instructions to fit the new circumstances, so that it must extrapolate for itself from new material presented to it but always within the framework of its old programming.

And the new material had come to it, chiefly, from what it heard . . . and much of that had come from the transmitter Baas had planted on me.

Well, there was no time for me to change that now, even if I'd had the know-how, which I didn't. But Hort could walk up to the android and it would not resist his taking the carbine from its hands.

I would have to go it alone.

"You," I said to Hort. "Over to the trunk."

He stared at me but he moved to the side of the upended trunk.

I set the masher beam to its narrowest angle, stood to the side, and sliced with it.

Sliced down across the hinges of the trunk to the sound of gasps.

Like a keen knife the beam could cut, and it did, and the hinges fell free to the floor, first the one . . . and then the other.

The back of the trunk was unsecured. It could be spread open now to pivot on its catches, its lock.

"Open it," I said to Hort. "Shove it open from the back."

"Are you insane?" he threw at me. "It is keyed to explode the moment it is tampered with. The hinges. I do not know why it has not gone off already. I will not touch it."

"No!" Brigit's gasp and Plagiar's weak shout had mingled with and been almost lost in the sound of Hort's protest.

"Open it," I said.

Our eyes locked. Locked and held and I was bringing up the muzzle of the carbine when I heard a smashing outside the door.

"Pike," I heard, and I recognized the voice of the corporal.

"In here," I said, and my relief at hearing the stocky corporal's voice was mixed with my chagrin at having failed to do what I felt must be done.

"You got here more quickly than I expected," I said to the corporal when the room was swarming with his men.

"We were already on the way when we got your call," he said.

"How?" I wanted to know, thinking of my wrist-chrono emptied of its transmitter and my communication with the corporal cut.

For an answer he plucked from his ear the small, antennaed shell of a receiver. He felt my left sleeve. "Your small camera, where is it?"

And when I had retrieved it from the floor behind the upended table, he held the receiver close to it and I heard the beginning of feedback; the unmistakable high-pitched protest of a receiver too close to its transmitter.

"When we found the packet of transmitters on Sklar, I took advantage of the opportunity to plant a second one in your camera." The corporal smiled. "I did not mention it at the time for fear that knowing of it might inhibit you."

And the corporal's sitting duck had led him to the killer of Baas.

Sklar.

It had to be Sklar.

Sklar, feeling secure that Baas was keeping Plagiar and the trunk and the boy away from each other, coming to Baas for a pigeon. Sklar, who knew Rook's son and who would know the instant he laid eyes on the android how Baas had tricked him.

Know and be furious . . . and in that fury kill as he had killed before.

And then, his fury spent, would realize that Baas had made his plan work all the better, and that now he, Sklar, alone knew that the boy was still back at the start of the trail.

That he need only find another decoy to send Plagiar after while he, Sklar, backtracked. And that decoy he knew he had when his and Brigit's plan to have me kill Plagiar missed.

A decoy who needed only a little play-acting on Sklar's

part to become colored with the appearance of authenticity.

Play-acting. Like pretending to be convinced with the others that I was Baas' accomplice and my knowledge of the boy's whereabouts might be bought with all his money ... and yet, after finding the transmitters, not wholly sure that I wasn't.

All his money drawn to prove his sincerity; only half of it offered to me because he needed the rest to run when he was ready, and he could not trust me not to pick it up and run on my own no matter how little I knew.

Play-acting to convince the others, and in the course of it and his need to be sure about me, getting his head bashed in by Hort.

I nodded at Hort, at Plagiar, at Brigit, all guarded by the corporal's men.

"What will become of them?" I asked.

The corporal shrugged. "Plagiar? I cannot say. But the one called Hort is right. They will hang together, he and she."

I looked at the trunk. "You know what is in the trunk?" I said to the corporal.

"Yes. I know what is in the trunk." He looked at me. "You knocked the hinges off. Why?"

I did not answer him, but kept looking at the trunk. "Can we open it?" I said. "Alone?"

He took a long time answering and when he finally spoke, his voice sounded as though it were coming from far away. "It can be arranged."

And when, under his direction, the room had been cleared and the prisoners moved to the anteroom, he came back in and closed the door behind him.

"I will help you," he said.

But with his hand on the trunk he hesitated. "Why are you so certain that it will not blow us to the sky the instant we spread its sides?"

"I never met Rook," I said. "But no matter what story he told to keep people from nosing around, I don't see a man who could worry himself half out of his mind that what he'd stumbled onto would hurt humanity, setting a trap to kill even one man, let alone whoever might be near him when he got curious about the trunk."

"You are sure of this reasoning," the corporal said.

"I would stake my life on it," I said.

"You are ... and mine as well."

And he bent his back and we shoved open the trunk.

EPILOGUE

Smoke layered the air of the room in wisps and shards. Red-eyed, the corporal batted at it with his hands.

"He was a one to keep many notes, this August Rook," he said.

I nodded. I had taken apart what I could of Rook's device, smashed with the butt of the carbine what I could not. Without the notes the corporal and I had burned, it could not be recognized for what it was, let alone reconstructed.

"You are almost finished?" the corporal said.

"Yes. The disk on the trunk, I've left that where it is. It's nothing more than an adapted bio slicer, and someone may have noticed it and would ask about it if it's gone."

The corporal nodded. "It is done then, and we will speak of this . . . you and I . . . to no one."

From the open window came the sound of a police vehicle approaching. The double high-low beeping of it should have sounded no different from that of any other. Yet this one had about it a certain imperiousness, a note of self-importance.

The corporal sighed audibly and redoubled his batting at the smoke. "It is the general," he said. "This promises to be a case of much importance. Plagiar is a big man, and we have not had a quadruple killing on *Poldrogi* ever before. The general has a long and sensitive nose and I would not wish for the smell of burned papers to intrude itself upon his thinking."

"Don't worry," I said. "If he believes anything of what Plagiar and Brigit try to tell him, you can always fall back on there being a thermal device in the trunk that went off and burned everything the instant the vibration from my carbine hit the hinges."

But all the same I got to my feet and started helping him swat the shards of smoke toward the open windows.